THREE DAYS
in
AMSTERDAM

a novel

Tanja Davia Tucker

This is a work of fiction. Names, characters, organizations, places, events, and incidents are either products of the author's imagination or used fictitiously.

Text copyright ©2023 by Tanja Davia Tucker.
All rights reserved.

No part of this book may be reproduced, or stored in a retrieval system, or transmitted in any form or by any means, electronic, mechanical, photocopying, recording, or otherwise, without express written permission of the publisher.

Published by Tanja Davia Tucker.

ISBN: 979-8-9866500-3-6 (e-book)
ISBN: 979-8-9866500-2-9 (paperback)

Cover and interior design by David Provolo.

First edition.

*For Pieter de Langen, my father,
whose perspectives always deepened
my life experience.*

Contents

1. Christmas Day Reflection 9
2. Broken 13
3. Beginnings 22
4. Take Off 34
5. Awakening 43
6. Strike One 55
7. Exposure 63
8. Strike Two 77
9. Discovery 84
10. Judgment 99
11. Stuck 111
12. The Shift 120
13. Back Again 133
14. Introductions 146
15. No Contact 157
16. Paper Trail 174
17. Bad Contact 190
18. Strike Three, You're Out 224
19. A Birth 235
20. A New Backbone 250
21. Christmas Day-Again 267

Book Club Discussion Questions 275
Acknowledgements 276
About the Author 278

"If you judge people, you have no time to love them."

—Mother Teresa

Author's Note

The inspiration for this fictional story came to me years ago, while I was in Amsterdam with my husband during the holiday season. While we were out strolling one night, we stumbled upon the Red Light District by accident. My initial reaction to our discovery surprised me—I was immediately uncomfortable, and a feeling of unease stayed with me long after we returned to our hotel.

In the days that followed, my discomfort shifted into curiosity. Unable to stop thinking about the Red Light District, I began to read articles about the evolution of this very old part of the city. I also found compelling stories about the sex workers who work there. No two stories were alike, but each offered a unique glimpse of the many ways in which people survive, cope, persevere, and succeed in this world.

This encounter triggered memories of my father. He was born and raised in Amsterdam. Over the years, when the subject of "the oldest profession" came up around him, he voiced an open-minded perspective. It didn't seem to fit. He lived a conservative life based on strict morals and expectations, so his view of this particular aspect of Dutch culture left me puzzled. Growing up, I struggled to understand his belief that the people who worked in the Red Light District were people just like us. "You should never judge someone until you know their story," he'd tell me. He wasn't the only Dutch relative who held this opinion, and I continued to wonder why so many people supported the Red Light District.

It wasn't until after I'd stood in the district, as an adult, and saw it for myself that I began to truly consider my father's viewpoint. From there, a story emerged.

Three Days in Amsterdam explores the lives of characters from different social and economic backgrounds and the stereotyping they must face. As she took shape on the page, Miriam became what I believe is the quintessential heroine—someone who refuses to let others' opinions define her. I became fascinated by delving into the dilemma her character offered: Was it possible to have a foot in two different worlds? More importantly, should she be judged by her profession or by her actions toward others around her and in need? As a reader, I like when a book ignites reflection of all sorts and a desire to gain more insight. While Miriam isn't the protagonist of this novel, it's her story that I hope will encourage readers to give thought to how many times conclusions are drawn and judgments are made about people without taking the time to learn their stories.

My first novel was dedicated to my mother. While writing this novel, I reconnected to so many childhood memories of visiting the Netherlands with my father. It was during these visits that I heard many discussions about the Red Light District, and I now credit my father for offering me a unique point of view that I felt was worth writing about.

And so, this story is dedicated to him.

1

Christmas Day Reflections

Is it possible to undo seventeen years of self-ruin with one impulsive act? I was about to find out. It seemed like something that could only happen in a movie. And yet, it was as if someone had grabbed a pair of my drugstore readers and replaced them with perfect vision. The clarity was startling, and with my heightened sense of sight, it was evident that there was no turning back to the blur of my former life.

In high school, I learned about a type of cicada that makes its appearance in the northeastern United States every seventeen years, like clockwork. Shortly after these cicadas hatch, they burrow into the ground and remain there until signaled by their environment to emerge. I guess if bugs can go dark for seventeen years, why not humans?

Standing in front of that glass door, I felt an odd connection with these insects. The difference was that my clock wasn't tied to environmental factors. No, mine was tied to matters of the heart—to a fine mixture of ugliness served up in a beautiful chalice meant to mask the sludge I'd been digesting. Over the course of seventeen years, so much of me had dissolved, broken down. The chalice had lost its shine.

Like the cicadas, I was about to resurface.

I considered the door I was facing. It was made of glass. While I knew that the term "glass ceiling" was generally used in reference to women being prevented from achieving at a certain level in the workplace, this glass door offered women all the potential in the world. It certainly had the power to change my life forever.

I welcomed the change but knew that everyone else in my weary little world would have far more contrary reactions. I could almost predict their words.

"Why would she throw away a perfectly good life?" my mother would lament, as she grieved the existence she'd so badly wanted me to live.

"Almost twenty years," my husband would say, his jaw clenched. "You'd think you'd know someone well enough to see this coming. No one will know about this if I have anything to do with it."

"She's in serious need of therapy if she thinks this is going to solve anything," my husband's colleagues' wives would say, finishing a bottle of wine.

"Oh my god, how embarrassing," my son would whisper

under his breath with contempt. "She's completely lost it."

The last one would sting the most. Just imagining it made me feel as if I had a yellow jacket stuck in my hair piercing my scalp repeatedly and leaving me aching for relief. I'd never get used to this painful impasse that had developed between my boy and me. And I'd never allow myself to imagine a life without him, regardless of what my husband proposed.

As far as everyone else who knew me was concerned, I didn't care. Some would see my actions as shockingly entertaining. Others would find them hard to digest. Regardless, I was a world away from all that now.

My expression, reflected in the glass door, was calm. My presence exuded a strength that had gradually evaded me over many years. It felt like a reunion of sorts: my old self encountering my new self after a long hiatus. I heard the universe greeting me.

Welcome back, Beth. You look great!

The first time I'd looked in the glass door, I'd seen what was on the other side and been appalled. Now, as I stood firmly planted, I saw everything around me, swirling in currents, a petri dish of life waiting to be examined. The image was fluid and ever-changing. It couldn't be held, only observed and appreciated or reviled. I decided to appreciate it.

And then, reflected in the glass—a pair of eyes not my own. They were blue, the color of a calm sea, and they latched on to my gaze, warming the very space where I stood. The power of the connection stunned me, yet I didn't turn around. Instead, I relied on my senses to carry me along.

I closed my eyes like an old cat and inhaled deeply. Then I opened them slowly as I exhaled. The other set of eyes hadn't disappeared. They were still there, patiently waiting. True to my new, reflective self, I paused to consider the possible effects of my choice. My next move held the promise that my life would never be the same. How could I go wrong?

I reached for the knob and, with no further thoughts, stepped through the door.

2
BROKEN

Earlier that month

Thanksgiving had come and gone, and I was feeling like the carcass of a turkey, picked over and discarded. I'd been holding out hope that the Christmas decorations would spark me back to life.

The holidays had always been a highlight of the year for me. Decorating was one thing that I could do well. It sounded sad when I put it in those words.

Normally, I took painstaking hours transforming our house into a Christmas wonderland. Each treasure had its place: The manger from Bamberg went on the piano, along with the two wooden angels playing horns and flutes from Frankfurt. The advent wreath from Würzburg always took the spot smack in the middle of the butcher block. The porcelain gingerbread house from Munich made its home on the windowsill in the dining room, as did the gnomes and prune dolls from Nuremberg.

My delft bell from the Netherlands hung in the kitchen, above the butcher block, and the greenhouse window above the sink was full of a variety of ceramic birds. Two reindeer, from Amsterdam, shared a spot with the birds as well as a bunny from Paris wearing a fancy Santa hat and two finely dressed mice from Strasbourg in red jackets with shiny gold buttons. All were positioned as if the observer had come upon them spontaneously while they feasted on an illuminated strand of berries and poinsettias.

While the decorations were international in nature, I was not. These global gifts were souvenirs that Dennis had bought throughout the years of our marriage and delivered to me in our home in Pacific Grove, California. His job had him traveling a good deal, and the holidays always seemed to take him to Europe—Germany, the Netherlands, and France, specifically. These trinkets were supposed to ease the pinch of reduced family time, of being unable to attend parties together. I'd never been to any of the places these treasures had come from, but the beauty of each gift helped me generate my own impression of Europe. And it was grand.

Everyone, meaning Dennis's work colleagues and their partners, always raved about our Christmas decorations, but this year, I couldn't even get these right.

I couldn't get the Nativity to look the way it should. The sheep kept falling over, no matter how I positioned them, and this caused a chain reaction among all the animals milling around the manger. The wise man holding myrrh kept leaning over Joseph as if he had a secret to convey.

Meanwhile, in the kitchen window, another calamity was occurring. I couldn't get my animals to appear engaged in the berry garland. I almost dropped my delft bell as I was hanging it. Everything was off. What usually offered a rush of joyous inspiration seemed like labor. It was as though I'd unwrapped foreign objects and was standing in the wrong house.

What was the point?

I hadn't been myself since the accident. Someone had pressed the pause button on my life, paralyzing my senses and feelings. My body moved around, but inside, I was frozen. I breathed in and out without regard, thus perpetuating my pathetic existence.

I'd brought to life this Christmas transformation for seventeen years. I should have been able to do it in my sleep. Wasn't this my purpose in life, after all? To create the illusion of joy and contentment?

Shamed filled me. *Get it together, Beth.* Around me was the house that I'd once believed existed only in my dreams. Never in my wildest imaginings had I thought I'd live in such a grand place: Forty-four hundred square feet of perfect hardwood floors with mahogany accents. Four bedrooms with immaculate cream-colored carpets and crown molding highlighting every nook and cranny. A master bathroom, accented with marble and art deco fixtures, that was bigger than the apartment my mom and I lived in for most of my childhood. Big windows that offered a view of the manicured yard. A wraparound porch that spilled into a garden with shaped topiaries and roses. I'd always reaped such joy as I secured the tall plastic candy canes on the brick walkway and positioned the Christmas wreath perfectly on the walnut front door.

Despite all these things I should be grateful for, I couldn't summon any motivation to turn our house into a winter wonderland, a Christmas castle, a yuletide sanctuary. This year, our house seemed more like a dungeon, a jail, an exile.

Ahead of me loomed another holiday season with my husband gone, half a world away on a business trip. I just didn't know if I could rally myself to create the Christmas illusion just so that he could slip into the house the day before Christmas and be assured that I'd done all the shopping, sent all the Christmas cards, wrapped all the presents, baked all the cookies—handled all that was required of this holiday.

I couldn't blame the holiday for this sense of powerlessness. This loneliness. I could almost hear my son now, sounding exactly like his father: "Are you feeling sorry for yourself again?"

I returned to the kitchen to give the garland another shot. I leaned over to reposition the reindeer in the greenhouse window, but when I moved, the entire garland moved too. A piece had caught on my sweater.

My bunny from Paris bumped into the Strasbourg mouse, which knocked over the other porcelain reindeer from Amsterdam. Pieces went flying after hitting the granite countertop. One bunny ear and two reindeer legs landed on the kitchen floor.

That's when I started to cry—about the broken treasures or the reminder of the self-destruction that seemed to be in progress, I didn't know. Maybe about the berating I'd receive the minute my husband saw the damage. Or, perhaps, about the fact that I'd lost these reminders of a world that I'd only ever seen in my mind.

I cried on the kitchen floor for a long time. *What would my mother say?* I eventually thought. I knew immediately.

Get the glue.

Repairing the bunny was easy. The seam from the break was barely visible. The reindeer was a different story. Both front legs had broken, and the fit wasn't clean. Several crumbs of porcelain looked like they were beyond the point of rescue, the pieces too small to fasten cleanly, but I had to try.

Dennis walked in as I was sitting at the kitchen table reattaching a larger piece of a leg.

"What happened here?" he asked frostily, scanning the wreckage.

"I'm so sorry," I replied, setting down the reindeer gently to see if my glue job would hold. The trinket stood upright for a second and then hit the table, breaking its nose and an antler in the process.

The tears began again, and this time they were accompanied by small sobs that I couldn't control. I put my head down on the table and succumbed. And then the most unexpected thing occurred.

"Whoa, Beth," Dennis said, putting his hand on my shoulder. "It's just a silly reindeer. An expensive reindeer, granted, but I can get you another."

Shocked, I glanced up at him. He smiled. "Where did I get that one again?" he remarked, seemingly talking to himself.

"Amsterdam," I said with a sniffle. I made a point of remembering where every gift had come from as a way of honoring its uniqueness.

"Amsterdam. Ah yes. I remember now." He cleared his throat. "Well, I have to go there next week anyway, so I'll take a look. I'm sure these are common holiday decorations over there. I should be able to get you a replacement if time allows."

The reminder that he was leaving soon set me off again, and my sobs escalated to panicked whimpers. As hard as I tried, I couldn't control my emotions. *What is happening to me?*

"Oh, Beth, really," Dennis said, with uncharacteristic calmness. Who was this well-tempered man? "Settle down. This is nothing to cry about."

"Take me with you." The words came out before I knew what I was suggesting. They prompted a halt to my sobs.

"Take you with me to Amsterdam?" Dennis asked, frowning in confusion.

I'd never suggested accompanying him on a business trip in the entire seventeen years that we'd been together. Not that I wouldn't have enjoyed it. I'd just always assumed that if he wanted me to go, he'd offer. The offer had never come. There'd also been Troy to think of. He'd been in school. But of course, things were different now.

"Please, Dennis. Take me with you . . ." I knew I sounded desperate. I didn't care.

"Are you serious?" he asked, appearing to be emerging from his confusion.

"Yes. Oh yes. I wouldn't get in your way. I just don't want to be here alone."

He scowled slightly. "Well, you know, I have a busy schedule with this merger coming up, so you'd be on your own during the day. And I work through dinner sometimes."

"I know." I nodded eagerly. "I wouldn't care. Amsterdam would be a dream to see." Many times, I'd imagined myself walking through this city full of romantic canals, red-brick bridges, tall steeples, and cobblestone streets. My need to get away suddenly felt overwhelming. "Please, Dennis. I just don't want to be alone. I feel like I've been coming apart ever since the—"

"And you think a trip to Amsterdam will fix all that?" he interrupted sharply.

There's the Dennis I know, I thought. Still, I refused to give up.

"It couldn't hurt." I felt myself losing hope as I looked at his face. Tears filled my eyes again.

He picked up the broken reindeer antler and twirled it around in his fingers. "You know," he said, "it might not be a bad idea, given everything that's been going on. Being here alone might not be the best thing for you."

He paused and looked at nothing in particular. I knew he was thinking about the accident. I was familiar with that look. It was the one thing we had in common now. And then, as if some invisible force snapped its fingers and returned Dennis to the present, he resumed laying out his plan.

"I have to be in Amsterdam for three days and then Rotterdam for a week. You think you can keep yourself busy?"

"Oh, Dennis, I know I can." I stood and threw my arms around his neck.

He placed his hands tentatively on my waist. The gesture felt awkward. We hadn't touched each other like that in a very long time. "Well, let me check a few things and see if my secretary can convert some frequent flyer miles for me." I could see him running through his to-do list in his head. He pulled away from me. "Why don't you put those things back in the box and take a reprieve from this decorating madness."

This was all so unlike Dennis. He never missed an opportunity to acknowledge my errors, usually with sarcasm and a hint of anger. This Dennis seemed more like the man I'd married seventeen years ago. More thoughtful. Where had this Dennis been hiding?

"What about the managers' cocktail party?" I asked, just remembering. We hosted it every holiday. All the company big shots came over for drinks and appetizers and Dennis got to show off for his cronies.

"Pete's wife has been dying to get a shot at it," he said with a chuckle. "They bought that new house with the olive grove, and they've been hinting that if we wanted to take a year off, they'd be happy to host it. So let them!"

"I think that's a great idea," I said, giddy, feeding off his lightness. All those stuffed shirts in one room—it had never been my idea of a great time. The evening was always about one-upping and playful humiliation.

"OK, I'm going to change and then give my secretary a call. You go throw some water on your face and then put that stuff away. What's for dinner?"

3
Beginnings

The car had pulled into the driveway ten minutes ago, but Dennis was in no hurry. He loved to make his drivers wait. The driver eventually got out of the car and paced while talking on his cell phone. Then he leaned against the black sedan and picked at his cuticles.

I watched from the upstairs window, my bag zipped and ready, my purse close at hand. I'd decided to carry my coat instead of packing it, as I'd read that December in the Netherlands would be far colder than our California winter.

I knew better than to remind Dennis that the car was waiting. I always felt so bad for the drivers. One time, I'd offered a driver a peach from our tree and Dennis had come unglued. He'd told me in no uncertain terms to never do that again, that it was a pathetic effort to blur the lines. I didn't question him. He had numerous idiosyncrasies that seemed to make sense to everyone but me. But today I was going to Amsterdam with him, and nothing was going to get in the way of my excitement.

I watched him as he switched out pocket squares in his sports jacket and then added his comb to the toiletry bag. I stifled a chuckle—he really didn't have any hair left to tend. He'd had a head full of hair when we met seventeen years ago, although there was a suggestion of things to come in the area of bountiful bellies.

I'd met him at a company party, my first social event at my new job. It was clear he was a bigwig as he stood in a circle of men who seemed to hover on the very air he breathed. I remember thinking that the sound of the laughter coming from their circle sounded bottled. Timed.

When I asked my colleague Sheila who he was, she laughed at me. "That's Dennis, the world's oldest bachelor!"

"What do you mean by that?"

"Well, maybe not the oldest, but he's been with this company for a long time and he's one of the only men left at his level who isn't married. He gets ribbed for it." She lowered her voice slightly. "Although, no one really messes with Dennis." She looked over in his direction, and so did I. The men all had knitted brows now, so the conversation had likely turned to work.

"I hear he's being considered for the CEO position," Sheila continued.

She always had the scoop, even though she'd been

working there only four months longer than I had. I'd been hired, by a friend of my mom's, as an administrative assistant in the event-planning department, which was a fancy way of saying I helped set up company events. I'd jumped on the job because my two years at the local junior college were up and I wanted to save for further schooling. My mother didn't understand my pursuit of education. Plus, it required money we didn't have. When her friend mentioned a job opening, she'd insisted that I apply.

"This tech firm is a great opportunity, Beth."

I had no interest in the tech world. I wanted to teach or do something with the community. I'd always wanted to work with people, make a difference. I wasn't sure event planning qualified as making a difference. Still, it was a job for the time being.

"Bah," my mom had said once when I told her about my professional goals. "Do you know how much teachers make? Do you? Not very much. That's how much." Then she made a small sucking noise as she inhaled.

"So it doesn't matter if I'm not interested in my work as long as I make a lot of money?" I asked, already knowing her answer. My mom and I had always lived on a very tight budget.

"Absolutely, Beth!" she said, her eyes widening. "Let's not kid ourselves here. You'd do yourself a favor to keep those green eyes of yours open for eligible bachelors. You're not getting any younger."

"Mom, I just turned twenty-one!"

"Twenty-one now and before you know it, you'll be

thirty-two and alone, with flabby thighs and a belly." She grabbed her waist and pinched her belly fat. "Men don't like flabby women. Or wrinkles."

By the end of the week, I'd interviewed for the position and, with a good word from my mom's friend, secured the job.

West Tech Systems had grown quickly and become one of the big names in the software industry. My job, of course, had nothing to do with the techie side of the company. I had been groomed to perfectly place centerpieces and select appropriate tablecloth colors. I'd learned how to set up a dining room and seat people of importance toward the middle and at the front. I'd learned how to find the venues best suited for whatever event the company was having. People on my team told me that those in my position usually had a college degree in event planning. In my opinion, no one really needed to take on student loans and debt to learn the things I was learning, since I had no desire to go further with event planning and make it my career.

This first party was in celebration of the release of a new software app. My team of four and I had done our research, and everything about the room seemed to say "success," from the opulent flowers to the gift next to each place setting wrapped in the colors of the product's packaging. I was certain that none of those men in the circle noticed anything beyond their empty glasses, which they often dashed to the open bar to refill.

My boss had told me to dress conservatively so I'd be inconspicuous, but either I was being pranked or the rest of my team hadn't gotten the memo because they were dressed in evening attire that suggested anything but blending in: form fitting, plunging necks, high hems. Nevertheless, I felt comfortable in my knee-length little black dress with the high neck. My role at the party was to monitor and troubleshoot, not socialize and have a good time. This was something I was well practiced in.

In high school, I'd been a wallflower. I didn't date because my mom was paranoid when it came to boys' intentions, and I didn't attend the dances or proms because we didn't have the money for "frivolous expenses." One of the neighborhood boys had asked me to the junior prom, and when I shared the news with my mom, she shot it down quickly.

"The prom? With Benny? That sounds like a waste of time."

"Why do you say that?" I protested. "The theme is Moulin Rouge! The art department is even making a replica of a windmill as a backdrop for pictures."

She scoffed. "That's horrible. Moulin Rouge? That's where men go to fulfill their fantasies."

I frowned in confusion. "What? It's a cabaret in Paris. Our English teacher told us it's a love story based on a Greek tragedy."

"Well, your English teacher must be a man. Boys your age don't need a suggestive theme like that. They already have all those hormones built up with nowhere to go. Anyway," she said, waving her hand dismissively, "you and I can watch a romantic movie and make some popcorn and save a lot of money. Dresses are pricey, you know, and then you have to buy a boutonniere. I also heard that sometimes the boy expects the girl to pay for her dinner . . ." She left her comment hanging, as if to accentuate the absurdity of the idea.

"So I can't go," I said glumly. It wasn't a question.

"Not this time." With that, the discussion was closed. I never got asked again. No one wants to risk being turned down in high school. The gossip can be cruel. I felt bad for Benny. He never talked to me again.

Growing up, I didn't have many friends because I was embarrassed to invite them over. My mother was not very keen on having strangers in our apartment either. My mom and I lived in Sand City, while most of the kids at my school lived closer to Monterey, where life was more upscale.

"Where's your drink?" Sheila asked me incredulously, as if I'd forgotten to put on underpants.

I turned to face her. "I wasn't sure if I was allowed to?"

"Oh Beth. Dear naïve Beth. Of course you can. You're not a servant. You're part of the event-planning team, and our work is almost done. You just need to keep your drink on the back table, out of sight." She gestured toward a table in the corner. "Now, what will it be?"

She grabbed my elbow and led me to the bar, where I ordered a margarita.

"What kind of tequila would you like?" the bartender asked.

I was out of my element.

"She'll have Patrón, right, Beth?" Sheila said, coming to my rescue.

Moments later, the bartender handed me my drink. I glanced at the large glass bowl on the bar. It had already collected a hefty number of five- and ten-dollar bills. I had a sudden urge to stick my hand in there and grab hold of a day's wages. That kind of money could have bought me a ticket to a concert, a dinner at a nice restaurant, a pair of stylish shoes, a haircut at a decent salon.

"Was I supposed to tip him?" I asked Sheila, as we walked away.

"Oh no. Leave that to the suits. They love to put money in that bowl to remind themselves how wealthy they are." She nodded toward the circle of men, which had grown.

As the evening progressed and I watched people enjoy themselves, I felt a flush of pride for the work I'd done helping to create the event. I wasn't half bad at this! It wasn't work I wanted to do forever, but it felt good to see that I'd contributed to this successful evening.

After dinner, the CEO got up on stage and gave a speech about the new product and the company's vision. "We're all part of this great moment in time," he said, as if the company had just landed a man on the moon. It seemed a bit dramatic, but the suits all nodded and gave him a generous round of applause when he finished.

Then Dennis was called up to the stage. Taking the microphone, he looked confident and self-assured. He broke the ice with some light humor and made me feel immediately invested in whatever he was about to say next. He spoke of his department's hard work in bringing the product to life and offered his team many accolades. And then he did the funniest thing—he got down on one knee, looked at the table where his team sat, and said, "Without you, I'm nothing." The room exploded in laughter and raucous applause as he returned to his seat.

"That was really good," I said to Sheila, who sat next to me at the back table.

"He's really something. So humble. No one can understand why he's still single." She looked at me and grinned then nudged me with her elbow. "Too bad he's twenty years older than I am, or I might make a play."

We both laughed. The thought of being with someone that much older seemed comical. Why would someone as accomplished as Dennis be interested in anyone young and naïve?

Near the end of the evening, I returned to the bar to replace my drink, which had been eagerly bussed. The glass bowl on the bar was almost overflowing. After I ordered another margarita with Patrón, someone behind me said, "Steve, give the lovely lady your most-expensive tequila, please."

The bartender reached for a black bottle etched with silver. It looked fancy. Expensive.

I turned around and there was Dennis, a smirk on his face. "See if you ever go back. They always have this on hand for me. If you don't like it, I'll drink it. I'm Dennis," he said, extending his hand. "I'm not sure we've met?"

I took his proffered hand, hoping mine wasn't shaking. "I'm Beth. I just started with the company a few months ago."

When my margarita was ready, I grabbed it from the bar and wished that I had my purse so I could tip the bartender, despite what Sheila had said, but Dennis was on it. He dropped in a twenty-dollar bill, and I watched it land, held up by the fives and tens like those singers who fell into the crowd and let themselves be carried by people's outstretched arms.

"So, Beth, what department do you work in?" Dennis asked.

"I work on the event-planning team," I said, and quickly added, "It's been a really great experience. I love this company." I took a sip of my drink and wondered if I'd sounded like a suck-up.

"Most people do," he said with a smile. "So, how's that margarita? Can you taste the difference?"

"Oh yes!" I nodded eagerly.

"A lot smoother, right?"

"That's exactly what I was thinking!"

I smiled at him, and his eyes seemed to assess my whole being.

"Excellent," he said. "At least I've done one good thing tonight. Nice to meet you, Beth."

He turned and walked away, and I found myself standing there watching him as I sipped my drink. To be honest, I couldn't taste the difference, but I did go home that night and look up the tequila. The bottle I'd seen sold for seventeen hundred dollars. Its grandness had been wasted on my humble palate.

A month later, I got an email from a Mr. Dennis Strum. When his name popped up on my screen, I was knee-deep in organizing an employee-recognition lunch.

It took me by surprise because I hadn't run into Dennis since the launch event.

Beth,
I'm having a holiday cocktail party for my department and your boss suggested that you'd be the perfect person to help me make it a success. I'd need you to plan, organize, and be present to orchestrate the event. Are you interested?
DS

Stunned and confused, I immediately showed Sheila, whose desk was next to mine in a sea of cubicles, and her eyebrows turned into two curved caterpillars.

"Should I do it?" I asked.

She laughed. "Of course you should!" She looked back at the screen to reread it. "You must have made quite an impression on him. He always handpicks employees to help at his private events." Her caterpillars wiggled at me.

"I didn't realize I'd made any impression!" I said, my ego feeling stroked.

And so, I did "orchestrate" that cocktail party. Dennis didn't make a move on me. Nor did he on several occasions after when our paths crossed at work functions. He was always polite and respectful, so different from the guys my age who seemed unable "to keep their junk in their pants," as my mother always warned. I liked his maturity. I found it very attractive, actually, so the fact that he was twenty years older than I was faded within the bigger picture.

Finally, a few weeks after the cocktail party, Dennis

started asking me to accompany him to various events. I'd eagerly accept the invitations. He was very charming, always opening my door, pulling out my chair for me, and getting me my drink of choice. I'd sit quietly and listen to the men talk as the other women would head to the bar and whisper to one another. I wanted to try to figure out the men's secret to success. I was swept up in their energy and the way they postured.

Then one night, after a work dinner by the Cannery, Dennis asked if I wanted to take a walk along the cliffs in Pacific Grove. We parked, and as I got out of the car, he offered me his jacket. The breeze off the ocean was cool. I draped it over my shoulders. The gesture made me feel special. We had only been dating for six months, but it felt like I had known him a lot longer since we saw each other at work every day in passing, as well as weekly outings with work colleagues.

"I've enjoyed getting to know you, Beth," he said, stopping along the path. He faced the ocean, and his hands rested on the railing that kept people away from the edge of the bluff.

"I've enjoyed getting to know you too." I didn't want to say anything that would make me sound stupid or desperate. In truth, I'd relished the attention, relished feeling part of something.

"I'm not a man of many words when it comes to things like this. I feel like actions speak louder than words." He rubbed his hands together. "Would you mind looking in the pocket of my jacket? I believe I have something that you might like." He glanced at me then returned his gaze to the water. I put my hand in the front pocket of his jacket and pulled out a small box. I tried to hand it to him, but he shook his head. "Open it. It's for you."

I opened the box, and a diamond ring stared back at me.

"I thought that since we get along so well, we should make this official." With that, he leaned over and kissed me for the first time. It was long and deep and caught me by surprise. My head was swimming and my heart was racing. "So what do you say? Want to make this official?"

It was more a business proposition than a marriage proposal, but I said yes, believing that this was a very good decision. My mother would be delighted that I'd found a well-established man that cared for me.

"Beth, are you ready?" Dennis asked, zipping up his suitcase.

I turned away from the window and looked at my watch. The driver had been waiting for fifty-seven minutes.

"Yes." I smiled and wheeled my suitcase to the front door, my excitement bubbling over. "I can't believe we're going!"

He placed a firm hand on my arm before I could open the door. "Let's get something straight, Beth. This is no big deal. You are my wife. Assume the position."

He opened the door and gestured for the driver to get our bags.

I checked myself so as not to embarrass him further.

4

Takeoff

"Cabin crew, please prepare for takeoff."

They were the sweetest words I'd ever heard.

It was my first transatlantic flight. My first time in Europe and my first time accompanying my husband on a business trip. I hadn't been this excited in years. The last time I'd flown had been on our honeymoon—almost two decades ago!

The day after the decorating catastrophe, Dennis had informed me that his secretary had been able to book me a seat in economy. My heart had swelled with joy.

"Economy was the best that she could find for you at such short notice." He looked at me as if this could be a deal-breaker.

"That's wonderful."

He raised an eyebrow. "My seat is in business class, so

we won't be sitting together." He continued looking at me, waiting to see if I had an opinion on the information.

"Just come back and see me sometime!" I said with a grin.

"Don't you mean 'Come up and see me sometime?' He referenced a line from a movie we'd watched together one rainy weekend, early in our marriage. Like most of our minimal "together activities," movie-watching had fallen by the wayside.

"You know what I mean." I'd winked playfully, but he'd peered at me uneasily, as if unsure how he should respond.

It wasn't a look I often saw.

I gazed at the back of Dennis's head, up in business class, shiny and round—a beacon reminding me why I was fortunate enough to be heading across the continent, across the sea to a place I'd only read and fantasized about.

Then the flight attendant pulled the curtain that separated three hundred other passengers and me from the elite who'd paid five times as much to sit in seats that became beds, drink champagne, wash their hands with warm towels before dinner, and feast on fancier food. They also had noise-canceling headphones and a bigger selection of movies and were offered complimentary booze until they nodded off. At least that's how Dennis described it. He traveled business class exclusively, and played it off as no big deal, but I was pretty sure that things on the other side of that curtain were a lot better than sitting between a woman with a bad case of halitosis and a gentleman who reeked of curry.

As the plane took off, I fought tears. Was I just excited?

Or was I also feeling guilty that I was leaving Troy behind? I reminded myself that there was nothing I could do about it. It was impossible to be with him now, and staying home would only make me sadder. It was out of my hands. I busied myself with a sudoku puzzle as our plane entered the clouds.

"Mommy, where's Barney?" The tiny voice across the aisle startled me. It sounded just like Troy's had when he was little. I looked over.

"Here you go, baby," his mother said gently, as she nuzzled his nose with a stuffed purple dinosaur.

"How long until we get there?" said the boy, who appeared to be about three or four. "Will we see Oma soon?"

His mother chuckled and ran her fingers through his soft brown hair.

"We have a long way to go, Thomas. Why don't you read a book to Barney? I bet he'd like that."

I couldn't seem to look away. Life had been so much simpler when Troy was that age. Life had felt good and positive and hopeful. Troy had been such a sweet child, and we'd loved reading together. A stay-at-home mom, I'd given him all my attention. It was what Dennis had wanted me to do, and I'd done so gladly.

I tried to return to my sudoku, but I kept finding myself glancing at the boy. Thomas had been the name I'd suggested when we were picking names for our son, but Dennis didn't want one that came from the Bible or could be shortened.

"If we name him Thomas, then people will call him Tom, and I hate that name. It sounds like the name of a plumber."

"Well, what names sound good to you?" I asked him, so happy to be awaiting our first child that the name wasn't something I felt tied to. It wasn't as if I had a strong male role model who'd inspired me.

"I like Troy. It suggests strength."

I nodded. "Or what about Nathan?"

"You want to name our son after a hot dog?"

Troy it was. I loved being a new mom. I loved everything about it, and I couldn't wait until Troy had a little brother or sister to join him. I was sure Dennis would too. I immersed myself in motherhood, and even though I was much younger than most of the women in our circle of friends, I attended every playgroup.

Across the aisle, little Thomas was on a roll, going through his repertoire of books, which included *Goodnight Moon*. That had been Troy's favorite. He'd even add dialogue, pointing to the things that hadn't been told "goodnight," offering equity to all the items in the room as he bid them a good sleep.

I must have been staring because Thomas's mother finally gave me a look that said *What's your problem?*

"Your son is so sweet," I said quickly, to ease her mind.

"Oh, thank you," she said, her face softening. "He loves to read." She tousled his hair. "Especially to Barney."

"My son loved *Goodnight Moon* too."

She smiled. "How old is your son?" She leaned forward to see who was sitting next to me. "Is he with you?"

"Oh no, he's sixteen. He couldn't make this trip." I left it at that.

The woman blinked with surprise. I was used to it. Most people didn't think I looked old enough to have a son in his teens.

"Well, enjoy your peace and quiet," she offered with a smile, and then turned back to Thomas.

Is that what this is called? Peace and quiet?

How quickly my mood had shifted from excitement to longing, and we'd barely left the ground.

After the meal service, Dennis came to see me. I was opening my cookie, wrapped in cellophane. He'd just finished a hot fudge sundae. He told me that he'd chosen the chicken in a mushroom and white wine sauce for dinner. I laughed as I thought of the overdone pasta with crispy edges that I'd pushed around in the tin tray.

"The chicken didn't taste good," he said, but I knew that he was just trying to make me feel better. I could imagine his plate, platter, whatever people in business class got, licked clean.

"So how's the flight been for you so far?" he asked. "Watch any movies?" He glanced at the people on either side of me and winced a little.

"Not yet. That's my post dinner plan." I wanted to point out the little boy and tell Dennis how his voice sounded just like Troy's. But I didn't. He wouldn't want to think about that. He was a master of compartmentalizing. His ability to disengage and hide had amazed me throughout our marriage. I'd told him this once, and he'd argued that he wasn't hiding at all, just focusing on more important things. He was also very good at making his points.

"Well," he said, "I'm going to watch a movie and then go to sleep. See you in the morning."

I watched him walk up the aisle and disappear behind the curtain.

"Is that your husband?" asked the lady in the window seat.

I forced a smile as her breath wafted over me. "Yes."

Her bottom lip jutted out a little. "Why aren't you sitting up there with him?"

"Oh, we booked this ticket for me last minute. This is the best they could find." I quickly added, "It works for me."

She scoffed. "Well, that wouldn't work for me! If my husband did that to me, I wouldn't be a happy camper." She shook her head and looked out the window and then back at me. "You must be a better person than me."

I put in my headphones, signaling the end of that conversation. I was well acquainted with my role in my marriage. I'd spent seventeen years perfecting it.

There'd been a time, after Troy started school, when I thought about going back to work, but Dennis had been quick to remind me that he worked so no wife of his had to. I'd accepted this, believing he was thinking of me and telling myself that I should be grateful to have a husband who looked out for my well-being.

With time, I realized that it had nothing at all to do with me. My not working was about his image, his prestige, his wealth, his ranking in the company.

Should I have pressed the issue? Would it have changed

anything? These were questions I'd stopped asking myself a long time ago.

I flipped through the movies and picked a sappy romance. I was a sucker for these types of films and rarely got to watch them. Dennis referred to them as "drivel." Not long after the movie started, I dozed off and had a dream about Troy.

He and I were skiing, celebrating his fifteenth birthday, under a bluebird sky. The snow shimmered like diamonds under the sun. It was just the two of us. We were laughing. He was in the lead, joyfully sending up sprays of snow my way. We came to an edge and looked down to see a snowy basin.

"Should we do it?" he asked me.

"You first," I said, and we headed in.

Suddenly, he disappeared. I called his name. He didn't answer. When I caught sight of the tip of his red beanie, I hurried forward to find him hanging on the edge of an icy crevasse that ran perpendicular to the hill. When I looked beyond him, all I could see was darkness. I popped off my skis in a panic, got down on my knees, and held out my hand. "Grab hold," I said.

I tried to pull him up, but my strength was no match for his weight. I dug into the snow and used my body as leverage, but I could not lift him. I felt my body break out in a cold sweat as I futilely attempted to hoist him up.

He looked up at me with angry eyes and said flatly, "You did this." Then he let go and fell silently into the abyss.

I woke with a gasp to find the man next to me staring at me with concern.

"Are you afraid of flying?"

"No." I swallowed. My hands were shaking. "I had a bad dream."

"I never sleep well on planes," the man said, in a meager attempt to comfort me. "Unless I take something that the doctor prescribes. Then I sleep like a baby, but the people around me aren't very happy with my snoring. I've received complaints, so I refrain from using my prescription."

I smiled and thanked him for not taking the pills, trying to lighten the mood.

Then I pulled out my Kindle and tried to read my romance novel, but all I could see was Troy letting go of my hand and falling out of sight. I settled for watching the benign screen with the little airplane that marked our progress.

When we finally landed, approximately eleven hours after takeoff, the curtain to business class was pulled open. I tried to wave at Dennis, but he was too busy ordering the flight attendant to help him with his carry-on.

"I hope you have a great trip," said Thomas's mom, catching me by surprise. The entire flight had caught me off guard. Everything out of my control had followed me across the ocean.

I looked at her. She was packing up Thomas's books and trucks and, of course, Barney.

"You too. I hope you have a great time visiting Oma. Your mother?"

"Yes, we haven't seen her in a year."

"Well, I'm sure it will be so fun for her to see how her

grandson has grown." I smiled and looked over at Thomas, who gave me a big grin.

The line in the aisle started moving. I looked for Dennis, but he'd already exited the plane.

"Mommy," I heard Thomas ask in his squeaky voice. "Who was that lady you were talking to?"

"Oh, that was just a nice lady sitting across the aisle from us."

"I think she liked my Barney! I liked her."

All I could think of was how much Troy would disagree with the little boy's sentiments.

5

Awakening

How can such a magical place actually exist? That was my first impression of Amsterdam. We'd arrived at night, and on the very short ride to our hotel, I'd kept my face pressed to the glass. The lights in the trees, the lights in the windows, the lights in the shapes of candy canes and stockings on the sides of the brick buildings, the lights on the arches of the canals—it all took my breath away. The shops were decked out with decorations, and the nip in the air added to the magical feel.

But when I woke the next day, it was pouring rain and I could barely see any of the wonderland that had greeted me the previous night. Dennis had already left for the office. He'd told me earlier that he'd be back around eight in the evening and that I should go have some fun exploring. He'd left some euros on the table for me, until I was able to get to a bank.

I made coffee in the room and ate the biscuits I'd put in my purse on the plane, feeling out of my depth, like a schoolgirl who'd never left her hometown.

As I sipped my coffee, I took in the room for the first time. It was modern and featured high-quality art, including a black-and-white photo of a cathedral along the canals and light fixtures that suggested a fusion of Pottery Barn and Restoration Hardware. These were the stores that "the wives" always talked about, so I'd made myself knowledgeable about their products to fit in. The bathroom was luxurious and roomy: soft towels, big mirrors, glass-block shower walls, big showerhead, and a separate bathtub.

Returning to the main area, I went to the window. The sky was so dark that it looked as if we'd skipped the daylight hours altogether. After finishing my coffee, I paced the room, checked the window, paced some more. I thought of those poor animals in the zoo that paced endlessly as people taunted them and snapped pictures. Thank goodness there was no one here to witness my lack of adventure, my voluntary captivity.

I turned on the TV, but everything of interest was in Dutch, so I pulled out my Kindle. It wasn't long before I was reminded of the dream I'd had on the plane. Immediately, I became agitated. My need to get out of the room intensified. I wanted to see Amsterdam. Still, the rain persisted. I showered and dressed so that I'd be ready to go when the rain eventually relented

Around two o'clock, it finally did. I went downstairs, and the concierge offered me an umbrella, which I accepted.

I proceeded out the revolving door only to realize I had no idea where I was going.

I went back in. "Can you help me?" I asked the concierge. "I'd like to take a walk and see a bit of the city."

"Why of course. What would you like to see?" he said, in perfect English. "This might be a good day for a museum." He unfolded a map of the city.

"Are there any museums close by? I'd like to walk."

"Of course, madam. The Rijksmuseum isn't far. It has an extensive collection of Rembrandt and Vermeer if you like that kind of art. So much art could keep you busy for days! Or you might enjoy the Van Gogh Museum, behind the Rijksmuseum. It is much smaller and offers an exclusive selection of artists. There is also an outdoor ice rink between the two during the holidays. Although, this rain might make ice skating a bit difficult." He smiled and looked at me, waiting.

"What would you recommend?" I asked pathetically, unable to decide. Quite frankly, I was petrified to step beyond the revolving door, but I was more afraid of brooding away in the hotel room.

"That is difficult to say because everyone has such different tastes, but I'd recommend the Van Gogh Museum. Then, if you want more of the classics, you can go to the Rijksmuseum another day. The line for the Rijksmuseum will be very long now. I always tell our guests to start early when going there. It houses all the Dutch master painters. It is the equivalent of your Metropolitan Museum in New York."

I knew the comparison was supposed to mean something

to me, but all it did was make me feel stupid. I was a girl in a woman's body, with no worldly experience. I'd never even been to New York, let alone the Metropolitan Museum.

"OK, can you show me the way to the Van Gogh Museum then?"

And so, out I went into the afternoon. It immediately began to drizzle, so I had to use my umbrella, which made it hard to hold the map. Self-doubt took hold. It was familiar these days. I'd never been as tentative and insecure as I was now, at the age of thirty-eight. While lots of women my age were attempting to lose weight, I was losing myself. It had been happening gradually, year after year, as I portrayed the happy wife of Dennis. Seventeen years ago, I would have seen this day as a great opportunity to explore. Now, I stood petrified of the unknown, listening to the rain on my umbrella, as if it had the power to melt me away to nothing. *What happened to me?*

"Madam."

I startled. It was the concierge.

"I'm afraid that my directions have confused you."

He'd obviously witnessed my inability to proceed. And now he was standing out in the rain with me.

"Oh no, it wasn't your directions. It just started to rain and I . . ."

"Of course, madam, this is not good weather to meet Amsterdam on foot for the first time. Can I call you a taxi?" He looked at me with sincere concern, and it made me want to cry.

I shook my head. "I think I'll grab a bite to eat. You

have a restaurant in your hotel?" I asked.

By the way he looked at me, I knew that my question was a stupid one.

"Of course, madam. I will show you the way."

And so went my first attempt to see the city. Inside, I had a bowl of soup and some delicious thick-crusted bread. Trying to lose myself in my meal, I ordered a dessert and took tiny bites. The almond paste tickled my tongue. I wasn't sure what I'd ordered, but it was like a small flattened pastry filled with marzipan. I loved it.

My empty plate signaled the overeager server, who retrieved it and offered to bill my room. That was a relief because I didn't have enough cash to cover what I'd ordered.

Just another example of how inexperienced I was.

I went back upstairs, all desire to explore gone. I sat by the window and watched the sky grow ever darker while glancing through the magazines on the coffee table, admiring the European fashions. Everything seemed so sophisticated here, from the magazines to the concierge, and the suits and heels. I fantasized about strolling down the street in a long, narrow skirt, a coordinated blouse, and a matching jacket topped with a trench-coat-style raincoat. I'd look just like the long-legged lady on page 127. My heels would click on the sidewalk and my umbrella would rest on my shoulder. Back home, everything was casual. No one dressed up in heels and skirts to go shopping. I couldn't remember the last time I'd seen a woman wear a skirt or suit. My job was to fit in, not to stand out, so I dressed like the other wives, mostly in athleisure wear. Come to think of it, I didn't particularly like my clothes. They served a purpose. They allowed me to blend in.

I must have dozed off because when I looked out the window, it was dark as night. I glanced at my watch—only four thirty.

Should I try to go out again?

What would I tell Dennis? I couldn't tell him that I'd been too scared to walk around on my own. He'd never ask me to join him again. For my own self-worth, I had to go outside and see something. I couldn't bear the thought of Dennis ridiculing me for staying in this hotel room while Amsterdam teemed with life around me.

Before I could talk myself out of it, I grabbed my raincoat and headed downstairs. It wasn't a glamorous raincoat like the ones in the magazine, but it would keep me dry. There was a new concierge behind the desk. Having no desire to be humiliated again, I quickly grabbed one of the complimentary umbrellas, pressed myself through the revolving door, and headed in the opposite direction of the museums. It was too late in the day to take in art and so a nice stroll would offer me a chance to get my bearings.

At a busy street in front of me, with the train station to my left and canal boats up ahead, I took a right.

I'd accidentally left my map upstairs.

A phone would have come in handy, but whenever I suggested getting a cell phone, Dennis shot down the idea, stating that we had a landline. There was no need for me to have a cell phone since my place was in the home. I rarely went out without him unless it was to the dry cleaner or the grocery store and play dates.

Determined to make something of this opportunity, I devised a scheme. In my geography class in junior college, the professor had said that you could find your way in most cities without a map if you counted your blocks. And so, I decided I'd walk in a big square and avoid referencing the street signs with names that I couldn't even begin to pronounce: Prins Hendrikkade, Oude Waal, Geldersekade. I'd cross four streets and then turn right, and then cross another four and turn right, and so on until I returned to the hotel. Nobody would know that I was so ignorant that I had to use a primitive navigation method!

Before my self-esteem could plummet further, I forged ahead.

Throngs of people were heading over a quaint bridge into a pedestrian area, where cobblestones replaced the asphalt of the busy street. I'd crossed three streets when I decided to join them. Relieved to be away from the cars and buses, I lingered on the bridge and looked into the inky water below. The brick facades of the buildings around me were reflected in the water and reminded me of the train set Troy had loved when he was young. It had included little houses of various shapes and sizes, and he'd set them up in a row along the track. Up ahead was the faint contour of a church with a dome. As I made my way in that direction, something wonderful occurred: I realized I was out in Amsterdam, all by myself, at dusk, and nothing bad was happening to me.

Bravo, Beth. Baby steps.

The area was popular. Crowds of people swarmed the tiny streets lined with shops. The energy was vibrant. I'd seamlessly shifted from panic to exploration. The window of a cheese shop was decorated with wheels of cheese in the shape of a Christmas tree. Another shop had a sign that said *MAGIC MUSHROOMS*. Its window was full of marijuana paraphernalia entwined in holly branches; roach clips were attached to the branches like ornaments. A young girl walking ahead of me asked her parents, in English, about an item in a window. The parents seemed embarrassed. I looked to see a display of flimsy rubber containers that looked like condoms filled with candies.

I laughed. *What an odd thing to display.* I was well aware of how progressive the Netherlands was, though. Troy had always talked about how cool it was that pot was legal in the country. I'd never tried it so I really did not have an opinion, one way or the other.

As I walked, I was forced to take a right sooner than planned, so I mentally noted how this would affect my square. I found myself in a smaller pedestrian area that had a canal running through it, as well as a series of picturesque bridges that made it harder to navigate. Still, I felt a sense of abandon that I hadn't felt in a very long time.

Why were so many of my thoughts ending that way these days? "A very long time." It sounded pitiful. Tragically miserable.

I passed a whiskey shop that advertised fifty-year-old whiskey. Old wooden barrels were stacked in the window. Christmas elves, dressed in green and gold, sat along the edges of the barrels with their legs crossed. The shop was so full that people were spilling out the front door. Beside it was a bakery with an impressive array of sweets in the window, even at this late hour. People were moving with purpose in the compressed spaces. *I guess they have to*, I thought.

The next window displayed Christmas trinkets. I examined it carefully to see if there was a porcelain reindeer. There were lots of blue-and-white dishes but not a single reindeer to be found.

Well, it's a big city.

There'd be plenty of opportunities to hunt one down. I wondered if Dennis would remember where he'd gotten it. That might be a fun outing tomorrow. I'd ask him when he got back to the hotel.

I crossed another bridge and stopped at the sight of a canopy bed, complete with bedding and pillows, floating in the canal, beckoning weary travelers to lay their heads down and rest, if they dared to swim out to it. I wished I'd brought my camera.

Then, as I headed further down the street, I noticed another window. On the other side of this one was a woman in a very small romper sitting on a stool and seemingly feigning disregard for the fact that she was almost naked and lots of people were looking at her. Was this a show? Some sort of street performance? I looked around and down the street.

Realization struck me.

Oh.

It wasn't just one window but a block of windows, and in them were scantily dressed women—beckoning, pacing, calling, waiting. Outside, people walked by, some fast, some slow, some grouped together, some giggling. I'd stumbled into the Red Light District.

Anxiousness enveloped me. *I shouldn't be here.* I needed to go.

The streets were packed, and I became part of a mass that pressed itself forward like a human train. I tried not to look, but it was impossible not to see these almost-naked women behind the glass, lit by a red glow. From the corner of my eye, they looked like apparitions that dusk had set free.

A young, thin man wrapped in a scarf leaned toward me. "Do you have a light?" He spoke with a heavy Dutch accent.

"No," I answered curtly, preoccupied.

"Foreigners," he mumbled under his breath. He shook his head then peered at me. "You look like you've seen a ghost!" He smiled, but I couldn't read the tone of his voice. Was he just being nice? Or was he a total creep with ulterior motives?

Wow, I'd really been watching too much TV.

I picked up my pace, leaving him behind, growing more uncomfortable by the second. I'd once seen a special news segment about the Red Light District, and while I hadn't paid much attention to it, I knew that the area was one of ill repute—a place for shady dealings and questionable characters. Not a place for me. If Dennis found out, he'd flip. The last thing I wanted was to do something that would reflect poorly on him, although I was quite sure none of his colleagues would be strolling these streets to witness my presence.

Turning right, I stopped abruptly. In front of me was an enormous church, smack-dab in the middle of this chaos. A plaque on the side of it read *Oude Kerk*. Here I stood, by this beautiful house of God, and still I was afraid. Everything felt different now. Within the span of a block, I'd gone from feeling free to feeling afraid. I just wanted to get back to the hotel.

As I gazed at the church, I heard a rustling noise coming from a nearby alley, reminding me that I was on the edge of a devious part of town. Fighting the urge to break into a run, I headed down the street at a brisk pace. At least I had my umbrella if I needed a weapon.

I gasped as my shoe caught on something, and I almost fell flat on my face. When I looked down, I could see something shiny and rounded in the cobblestones. I poked at it with my umbrella, and it responded with a metallic clink. There wasn't enough light for me to make out what it was. Perhaps a grate covering a drain?

Wanting nothing more than to get somewhere better lit, I left the mystery behind. I crossed two more streets, took my last right, and exhaled. There they were, the hotel flags, up ahead. I'd gone out into the city of Amsterdam all by myself and survived.

For some, this might have been a meager attempt at an outing, but it had required characteristics that had been stripped from me over the years—traits such as independence and self-reliance. The outing had made it painfully clear how little of me was left in "the wife of Dennis."

Back in the room, I couldn't believe I'd been gone only

an hour. Settling myself at the window again, I thought about the energy of the street. I thought about the women I'd seen briefly in the windows—and I thought about my own sex life, or lack thereof.

Seventeen years. I'd been in sexual exile for seventeen years.

I'd stopped asking questions about it, stopped making the effort.

"What do you have to complain about, Beth? Look around you." It was my husband's most common response whenever I attempted to fill this particular void in our marriage.

Maybe tonight, I could make a run at breaking our seventeen-year dry spell. Maybe tonight was the night.

6

STRIKE ONE

D ennis entered the dark room well past eight o'clock. I was facing away from him but heard him sigh as he turned on the overhead light briefly. He turned it back off, likely noticing I was in bed.

I waited quietly, far from sleepy, while he was in the bathroom. I knew that I had to tread carefully. After all, it had been so long. I wasn't even sure how it all worked anymore.

He came out of the bathroom and slipped under the covers, but before I could turn around, he turned on the TV. He kept the volume low, and I was touched. Many nights he fell asleep, mouth agape, with the TV on at a normal volume. How had he found a news channel in English?

I didn't move, just lay curled up with my back to him, waiting it out. I'd waited seventeen years. I could wait a little longer. From CNN, he moved on to Premier League highlights of the week and then late-night TV. I let out a sigh and let my foot slide over to touch his leg. No reaction. No problem.

I continued to wait.

Finally, I heard the TV click off. He rolled over facing away from me, just as I'd suspected. I knew his routine. I had to move quickly now.

I rolled over and gently placed my arm around his waist. Warmth surged through me at the contact of our bodies, taking me aback. Even through his usual T-shirt and undies, I could feel the heat of his skin. It felt so electric, so charged with life. Dennis didn't respond. I let my hand drop a little, searching.

Instead of finding comfort, I unleashed a monster.

"What the hell are you doing?" Dennis flipped over and sat up. In the dark I couldn't see his face, but I knew it was full of outrage.

"I thought we could take advantage of this opportunity to be together," I responded quietly, trying to keep my heart from exploding out of my chest.

He reached over and turned on the lamp.

"Are you naked?" he asked, as he lifted the sheet. He quickly dropped it in disgust, as if he'd seen a mob of wriggling bedbugs. "What were you thinking? You know how I feel about you sleeping naked."

"I was thinking that you and I could find some comfort in each other."

His brow wrinkled. "Oh, is that what this is about? Troy? There's nothing that can fix what happened. Nothing.

You have to take responsibility for how you raised him."

This wasn't the first time he'd cast this type of disdain on me, nor the second nor the third. I'd heard this accusation dozens of times since the accident, and each time, a little more of me died. I knew there was nothing I could say to change how Dennis viewed the situation, so I steered the discussion back to us.

"I just wanted to be with you. I thought we could find our way back to each other." I reached out, but he batted my hand away, his expression cold.

"We've been over this before, Beth."

I remembered the scene in the kitchen, the response I'd received when I cried. In desperation, I let the tears flow again, hoping to appeal to his heart. "I miss you, Dennis. It's been so long, and I just want to be with my husband."

He seemed to consider my words then sighed and shook his head. "You never cease to amaze me." I knew this wasn't a compliment. "We are together. I'm right here. Plus, this trip might last longer than I expected."

"What?" I said, sucked into his shift in topic. He was a master of distraction and redirection. I accepted my fate.

I should have known better. My little excursion had allowed me to briefly think in unrealistically hopeful terms.

Dennis pushed off the covers and stood. "I'm going to take a shower. I have an early day tomorrow." He glanced at me. "I hope you have a nice day."

He left, and I lay there feeling as if a weight were pushing me down. I was like Gulliver when he woke in Lilliput, except the ropes that secured me were invisible. Ropes woven with feelings of unworthiness and lack of confidence, strengthened by guilt and fear. I couldn't even have a real conversation with my husband of seventeen years. How could that be? How had this happened?

It was as though my marriage had both begun and ended in the first year. From then, it had been a gradual unraveling of a life. Mine.

I heard the water beating against the glass doors of the shower and went to close the bathroom door that stood ajar, knowing he liked his privacy. With my hand on the knob, I glanced at the shower and saw Dennis with his back to me. He had one hand on the tiles and was leaning forward. He appeared to be washing himself with his other hand, but it didn't take long for me to realize that that wasn't what he was doing at all. I could see the tension in his back.

He'd once again taken matters into his own hands, quite literally this time.

I crawled back into bed, not worrying about hiding my sobs. So much for intimacy.

What's wrong with me? was the last thought I had before sleep rescued me.

When I woke the next morning, Dennis was gone. He'd left twenty euros on the dresser with a note: *For housekeeping.*

Money flowed freely from his pockets, whether it was for tips or for Troy. Many saw it as generous. Heck, I'd thought the same thing the night I met him and watched him put twenty dollars in the bartender's bowl. But now I knew that money was simply one of the tools that Dennis used to separate himself from others—a reminder that he was better than they were, and that if they wanted some of that money, they'd better respect him. Troy was a casualty of this.

In the beginning, I'd tried to reason with Dennis, pointing out that Troy didn't need four rented ponies at the party for his second birthday, or an expensive gaming system at three years old. Each time, I'd end up feeling like a terrible mother.

"Why do you want to deprive our son of the good things in life? Are you jealous of him? Haven't I given you a good home to live in and a life with no needs?"

On a material level, that statement was accurate. But money could never give me the things my heart needed. In the early days, I'd tried to talk to my mother about it, but she'd remind me of how lucky I was to be married to Dennis. "Most people your age don't have the things you have." Yet when I looked at the people around us who had much less, they seemed happy. My mother insisted that happiness was a state of mind and that I needed to change the way I was looking at it. I'd been so young and naïve. I'd listened.

I was almost twenty-three when Troy was born. He'd been conceived on our honeymoon, when Dennis and I were intimate for the first time. I'd never met a man like Dennis before, whose hands I didn't have to bat away, and it had been so appealing. I'd felt honored that he'd wanted to wait until we were married. Respected, even.

Our honeymoon was cut short because of an issue at work, so we spent more time flying to Fiji and back then we did in Fiji itself. It was the only place we'd made love in the seventeen years we'd been husband and wife. It was the only time we'd been away together. Until now.

Maybe that's why I'd gotten the wild idea to try to rekindle some romance.

A month or so after we got back from our honeymoon, I started experiencing morning sickness. It was the talk of the office. Everyone was patting Dennis on the back as though he were the stallion who'd bridled his mare, and he ate it up. People at the company made jokes about him supplying the company with a new generation of Strums to take over. They wagered on the sex of the baby. They wondered how big I'd get. And all the while, he beamed, loving the attention. I'd thought he was going to be a great dad and we were going to have a lovely family.

My ignorance and inexperience had me thinking that it was natural to not have sex while I was pregnant. Dennis would tell me that he didn't want to risk anything, and I accepted it without a second thought.

After Troy was born, Dennis continued to steer clear of intimacy, claiming that I needed to let my body heal. I was convinced that he had my best interests in mind and thought that it demonstrated incredible restraint on his part. My young body bounced back, and the months rolled by.

In those early months there were two more attempts at intimacy within the span of a few weeks, but things didn't work on his end. Both times, he slid out of bed wearing a mask of indifference, disappearing into the bathroom for a while, and coming out with his sweats on, as if to say,

"That's the end of that." Nothing was mentioned, nothing was discussed. After the second time, he made sure that whenever we went to bed, we were going to bed to sleep. Period.

I waited and waited for my husband to show interest. As Troy's first birthday came and went, I longed to be intimate with my husband. Finally, I broached the issue one evening as we lay under the covers.

"Dennis," I said tentatively. "Is there something wrong?"

"What do you mean?" he replied, as he rolled over to face me.

"It's been so long since we've been together, and I miss you."

He frowned. "Beth, we're together every day! I'm here right now, next to you. Why are you talking nonsense?" His words were filled with genuine frustration. "I gave you a son. Is that not enough? What more do you want?"

"Maybe a little sister or brother to keep Troy company?" I playfully suggested. Hope hammered in my heart. I'd been an only child and had always longed for a sister or brother who never materialized.

All emotion left Dennis's face. "Absolutely not. That door is closed." His tone suggested he was discussing a business matter, reminding me of his proposal.

"But . . . wouldn't you like another baby to complete our family?" I reached out to touch his chest, but he leaned back. My hand dropped to the mattress.

"I'm not sure how much clearer I can be than 'absolutely not.' How selfish can you be?" With that, he rolled over, ending the conversation. It was his signature move, I'd soon come to find.

I revisited the conversation when Troy turned two and again when he turned three and four. Each time I was met with the same response and no explanation other than an expression of sadness regarding how selfish I was. Maybe he didn't want another child disrupting his life? He was barely involved with Troy. Still, I held on to the secret hope that I'd soften Dennis to the idea of another child. I did my best to keep things light and show him the joys of parenthood.

Meanwhile, Troy became the mender of my loneliness and a source of constant love. We'd read for hours, build train tracks with his BRIO set, fill buckets of water in his plastic pool in the backyard. We'd color, build forts with chairs and blankets, eat lunch in his little tent. And when he'd put his head in the crook of my arm and drift off to sleep, I'd feel every moment of the transition, from his soft hair resting on my arm to the heaviness of his head as he let go and entered dreamland. I'd just sit and soak it in. It was the best thing ever. I loved to hear his breathing and feel his breath blowing the hairs on my arm. I learned to wiggle my fingers gently to keep my arm from going to sleep so that I could prolong the moment. These memories embedded themselves in my brain.

Now, on my second day in Amsterdam, my only option was to make new memories. On my own. I kicked off the covers and headed to the shower.

7

Exposure

"And where are you heading today, madam?" asked the same concierge I'd talked to the day before.

For the first time since our arrival in Amsterdam, the sun had come out, filling me with a renewed sense of anticipation and dispelling the reminders of my shortcomings as a woman. I was committed to finding more of the good things this city had to offer. Amazing how a little bit of sunshine can have such a positive impact. I'd taken in the edgiest part of town yesterday, by accident, and I was ready to see the beauty. Ready for all that Amsterdam had in store for me.

"Today is a far more inviting day to see the city," the concierge continued. "Amsterdam is at your fingertips."

I smiled. "Yes, I'm excited to see the city without an umbrella," I replied, eying the canister holding dozens of them.

He returned my smile. "Well, you should be able to enjoy a good portion of the day without rain, but the wind can be chilly, so button up." He reached for a map of the Old Town. "May I suggest a visit to the flower market? It is always a sight to behold." He highlighted a route on the map. "Just follow this and you will have no trouble finding it. But if you get lost, you may uncover an unexpected treat. Amsterdam is a lovely city to get lost in. And it is just as easy to get found."

I couldn't help inferring a double meaning to his words.

"That's good to know," I replied, feeling more and more confident.

"So you will be walking, then, or would you like me to call you a cab?"

"Oh no, I'm excited to get out and walk. Thank you."

As I headed toward the door, he called me back.

"You forgot your map!" He held it up. "Perhaps you like the notion of getting lost, but just in case, I've written the hotel's number on it for you. We are well known in the city, so anyone or any taxi will be able to get you back."

I thanked him again and headed out in the direction of the flower market. I was grateful to have the map this time, but the concierge was right—today, I wouldn't mind getting a little lost.

The air was cold, and the breeze made my cheeks feel fresh and alive. Inhaling deeply, I took in the activity around me. So many bikes. Bikes with baskets to carry groceries, bikes with child seats, bikes with saddlebags to carry work items, bikes with fancy bells to warn people of their approach. Rows and rows of bikes parked along the canals. Bikes locked against lampposts. Young girls riding on the handlebars of young guys' bikes. And where there were no bikes, there were brightly colored mopeds. It was like I had just walked onto the set of a European movie. I loved feeling part of it all.

Using the map as my compass, I followed his markings until I got to the Singel canal and then there it was, to my right: Bloemenmarkt, the flower market, floating on the canal. The concierge had told me that it had been around since the 1800s and supplied flowers to many places throughout the country. I could see why. It offered a wide variety of tulips, peonies, narcissi, snowdrops, and orchids. I discovered, after a few sniffs, that the tulips had very little fragrance; their colors and petals were the attraction. The narcissus and hyacinths made up for the tulips' lack of smell.

I soaked up the beauty of the many stands of cut flowers before beginning my pursuit of the perfect combination of bulbs to plant back home. Or, more precisely, for Miguel to plant—I wasn't allowed to tend the garden. At the register, however, I was met with bad news.

"Where are you from?" the old man serving me asked, with a heavy Dutch accent.

"America," I replied. "I can't wait to see these bloom in the spring." I held up the paper bag of bulbs and grinned.

The man shook his head sadly. "I cannot sell these to you."

My eyebrows flew up. What had I said? Was he not a fan of the American tourist? "I don't understand?" I must have looked crestfallen because he came around the counter and patted my back.

"Customs will not let you take these back. They will confiscate them and then you will have spent all this money for nothing." He shook his head again. "Many of the customs officers have some of the nicest gardens around thanks to the confiscated bulbs."

"How disappointing," I said. "And now I've mixed up these bulbs and made a lot of work for you."

He smiled. "This is not hard work for me. I would not be as cooperative if it were Saturday, but today it is slow. When it is the holidays, no one wants to buy bulbs. They want whiskey and cheese and lovely delft trinkets."

"Too bad. I really wanted to take home some authentic tulip bulbs."

"You can buy them in the airport, after customs. The colors are not as varied, but they come from the Netherlands."

I thanked the man, who went off to restock the bulbs. I was grateful for his honesty, and his act of kindness had me walking lightly despite my disappointment. I made my way toward the Van Gogh Museum to see if the line to get in was long.

I rounded the big brick facade of the Rijksmuseum, which looked similar to that of the central train station, where our driver had been waiting for us when we arrived in the city. I also spotted the ice-skating rink the concierge had told me about. There was a little white drawbridge over the rink, to make it seem as if you were skating on a canal. I sat on a bench nearby and watched several families skating.

Scarves and woolen hats adorned most heads and danced in the breeze. Some children skated with wooden chairs in front of them for support, and when they were tired, they just sat down. Brilliant! What a great idea. I'd never skated before and trying it out with a chair for support sounded more appealing and practical than trying to balance on a thin blade with no help. For a time in Monterey, an ice rink would be put in next to the wharf during the Christmas season, but the warm California winters made it a challenge to sustain. By the time Troy was old enough to skate, the project had been temporarily abandoned.

I thought of the time I took Troy to the roller rink when he was seven. He'd been invited to a birthday party there and was reluctant to skate. The mother hosting the party suggested that I skate with him and help him get comfortable. His eyes got all big and hopeful at the suggestion, so that's just what I did. We started on the outer part of the rink so he could hold on to the railing, and slowly we edged out and he got his skating legs.

Bravo, Troy! I'd thought with a smile.

When it was time to do the limbo, he called me over. "Mom, do it with me!" On the third round, I lost my balance and fell on my butt. He giggled and then skated out to help me up. "Oh, Mom, good try," he said, as he offered me his little arm.

We made so many good memories in those early years. He hadn't always disrespected me. No, he'd learned how to do that from his father—a slow, laborious, continuous lesson that started when he was about eight. Actually, the modeling had started earlier, but Troy had been too young and naïve to pick up on the caustic remarks and criticisms. He'd been oblivious to the fact that his dad wanted to be the singular figure of importance in his life. It's hard to be that person if you don't put in the time.

Unless you have the money.

When he was old enough to understand the muscle of dollars, Troy too, became seduced by it.

Oh my, here I go again, drifting into a maudlin place. Think tulips, Beth.

The line at the Van Gogh Museum looked manageable, and even though the sun was shining, the winter air had chilled my California body to the bone. Time to get out of the cold.

As I wandered through the multilevel museum, I got lost in the art, the history, and the drama of Van Gogh's life. *Better his drama than mine.* There were paintings by artists who'd inspired Van Gogh placed next to his works, and I appreciated this setup. It was perfect for an art novice like me, as it helped me to see the techniques the artists shared. I read every word on every placard.

Still, Troy was there with me.

The Bedroom at Arles reminded me of Troy's first big-boy bed. The first night he slept in it, I slept on the floor in his room. His little hand would reach out and he'd whisper, "Are you still there, Mommy?" I ended up sleeping there for three days, until I was convinced that he wouldn't roll out of bed. Dennis never asked me where I was and why I hadn't slept in our bed with him.

One of Van Gogh's self-portraits reminded me of the self-portrait that Troy did in first grade. His eyes were huge, his eyebrows were like the Frito Bandito's, and his hair resembled a roof. I loved it. I framed it and tried to hang it in our bedroom, but Dennis wouldn't hear of it, so I hung it in Troy's room.

Irises reminded me of a time when Troy and I went to a market together. I bought some irises for a dinner party that Dennis and I were having, and Troy said, "They're pretty, like you, Mommy."

Troy was everywhere. How was I supposed to just "forget about him," as Dennis had instructed me to do after the accident? He was my baby. My son.

A blast of cold air hit my face as I exited the museum, and the changed light made me curious how much time had passed. I also felt a strong pang of hunger which meant it was after the lunch hour. In all my attempts to distract myself, I'd forgotten to eat. I went back inside to ask the young lady at the gift shop if she could recommend a place to grab a quick bite. She directed me to the nearby Christmas market, which was close to the train station.

I soon found myself on a street filled with booths featuring handmade items and, according to the woman in the gift shop, the best wurst in Amsterdam. The wurst stall was quite a sight—clearly, I wasn't the only one who'd been told these sausages were good. As I stood in the long line, I saw that all the sausages were on a wheel-like grate suspended over a drum of fiery embers. The men working the booth were dressed in black and wore little black hats that looked like pincushions. The sausages were stacked in piles and separated by types in the shape of a pyramid. The men would pull from the bottom of the pile, and the other sausages would then roll closer to the grate, where they would cook. When an order was placed, they'd spin the wheel to find the type of sausage ordered.

Ingenious!

My opinion might have been clouded by the fact that I hadn't eaten in hours, but I thought that it was the best sausage I'd ever tasted.

Afterward, I strolled down the street of wooden stalls and admired the holiday crafts. On display were handmade mittens, hats, scarves, wooden toys, candles, candies, cookies, and Nativity statues. Holiday music drifted from many of the stalls, and I could feel my spirits lifting. *Look at me*, I thought. I'd been to the flower market, the skating rink, the Van Gogh Museum, and the Christmas market—all by myself. Once again, confidence tickled my senses. Maybe this trip would offer more than simply an escape. Maybe it would help me climb out of the chasm in which I'd been allowing myself to reside.

In the near distance stood a church with a tall, ornate steeple. I noticed several similar church towers on my walk the previous day. Maybe I'd see if it was open to the public.

My mother had taken me to church a few times after my dad left, in an attempt to offer me a good life. She'd tell me to listen carefully, but throughout the service she'd keep her head down and bite at her fingernails. She never talked to me about the service afterward. I was sad when we stopped going. It offered a sense of tradition I longed to be part of.

At eight years old, I never could have imagined a scenario in which one of my parents would leave. I had no reason to believe anything was wrong. Yes, money was tight, and yes, my dad struggled to keep a job, but he always found another one. We were never hungry or homeless. I don't have any memories of spending time alone with my father because he was always working or looking for work and then there was the local bar that he would visit regularly. I did hear my parents' raised voices coming from behind closed doors from time to time but never concluded that an end to our family as I knew it was coming.

One day he was there and the next he wasn't. My mother informed me that my father had left and wasn't coming back. She never offered any explanation or showed any remorse, so I tried to follow her lead, even though I was sad. While my dad and I were not close, his presence in our house made it feel more like a home. Without siblings, everybody mattered. We never talked about him again. In my early teens, I tried to ask her about him a few times, but she'd just shake her head, put her hand up, and walk out of the room. Whatever had transpired, she wasn't interested in rehashing it. It was as if my father had never existed. I never heard from him again. Never received any checks in birthday cards. I learned to write my father out of our family story. It was a lesson in how tenuous life was.

The sun peeked out from behind the heavy clouds every now and then as I headed in the direction of the church, and it was in one of those bright moments that I noticed light bouncing off a spot in the cobblestones. Getting closer, I could see that it was reflecting off an uneven metal surface. Maybe brass or bronze? It wasn't until I was standing right over it that I realized it was a sculpture embedded in the sidewalk—a sculpture of a hand caressing a naked breast!

"Interesting, no?" said a voice with a unique accent.

Flushing, I turned to see a young woman walking toward me carrying a bag of groceries and an enormous bouquet of flowers composed of lilies, tulips, peonies, hyacinths, and more.

"Oh, did you get those at the flower market?" I blurted, hoping to mask how awkward I felt. Had she thought I was gawking at the sculpture?

She smiled. "Yes, it is my biweekly errand. I like to gather the beauty and spread it around."

She looked like a model from the magazines I'd been flipping through: plaid skirt, dark sweater, heavy stockings, trench coat left open, and an angora beret that set off the highlights in her shiny brown hair. And those boots. I was a sucker for boots, and these were stunning. Black leather knee-high boots with heels and beautiful curves and contours that fit her legs as if they'd been made specifically for her. Black fur peeked out at the tops, suggesting that in addition to stylish, they were warm and toasty. She looked important. Refined.

I felt a twinge of envy. She was so confident, so beautiful, so well put together.

"Do you find it offensive?" she asked, as she nudged her bag in the direction of the sculpture.

I glanced back at the sculpture. "No," I said, bh again. "I wouldn't say offensive but a bit . . . unusual." I caught myself before saying "weird," not wanting to sound ignorant or disrespectful.

"Well, it gets a lot of reactions, that's for sure." She tilted her head toward the sun. "Look how God is shining down on her."

I followed her gaze and saw the sun's rays reflecting off the metal with such brightness that I had to look away.

"Who put it there?" I asked. "Was it for a specific reason?"

"It is a funny story. It was put there secretly, some twenty years ago, in the wee hours of the night." She paused. "Other sculptures by the same artist have popped up all over Amsterdam."

"Are they all like this?"

"No, but would that be a problem?" she said, regarding me. "It is beautiful, is it not?"

"Oh yes," I said quickly. "I didn't mean it that way."

"I know that everything has to have a meaning for you Americans. I get it." She grinned. "Actually, this sculpture represents the women of this part of the city. Come over here." She beckoned and began walking. Not sure where she was leading me, I found myself following her without question, fully intrigued, welcoming her interest in me.

As we passed the church, I noticed a plaque on the side of it: *Oude Kerk*. She must have read my mind because she remarked, "This is the oldest church in Amsterdam. *Oude* means 'old' and *Kerk* means 'church.' Not very original."

Realization struck. I'd passed this plaque when making my way back to the hotel the previous evening. Could it be that I'd tripped on the sculpture and not a metal grate? I looked around. Everything was so picturesque, like a postcard. Last night, everything had seemed so dark and macabre. Was this really the same street I'd stumbled on only hours before?

"Have you been inside yet?" the woman asked me, gesturing to the church.

"No, that's what I was on my way to do. It looks beautiful."

She nodded. "You should definitely spend some time in there, but first, come see this." She walked around to the front of the church, where we came upon another bronze statue. This one was on a pedestal, as statues normally are.

"Is this by the same artist?" I asked, studying it.

"No, this is the first and only statue made by Els Rijerse. It is called *Belle*."

The statue was of a woman standing in a doorway. I assumed she was a warrior—she had her hands on her hips and exuded a sense of independence and power.

"Does this date back to something historical?" I asked, peering more closely at the statue.

The woman chuckled and shook her head slightly. I flushed again. She probably thought I sounded stupid. "It was created in 2007, though I guess you could call it 'historical.' Make sure you check out the church and then go down this street. It will all make more sense."

With that, the woman smiled at me then whirled around and walked off in the direction she'd pointed. Her flowers and her bag swung in her arms as if they were alive, and the click of her boots on the cobblestones spoke of self-assurance.

Wistfully, I watched her walk away.

I was touched that she'd taken the time to share some of the city's art with me. I could only hope that my ignorance hadn't scared her away.

It cost thirteen euros to visit the church, but it was worth every penny. I'd never seen a structure so magnificent. It was like every castle I had seen, morphed into one. The high ceilings, the pillars, the stained glass, the massive altar, the ornate organ, the carved wooden pews—it all took my breath away. I found myself wishing I'd asked the woman to join me, so I could learn more from her. She'd seemed so knowledgeable.

The sound of the cathedral's doors opening and closing created a sense of infinity. It was easy to believe that God could live within these walls. *I wouldn't be surprised to see angels darting around through the pillars*, I thought, gazing up. This place felt holy, nothing like the church I'd briefly attended. That one had been more like a gathering room than a grand place of prayer. No statues or pieces of art, no stained glass windows or intricately carved pews. I'd had no idea that churches like this existed.

I took a seat in a pew, which let out a creak, and looked up, admiring the arches and angles above me. I felt a sudden urge to pray, and Troy came to mind. I closed my eyes, hoping to see his face, but all I could see was my son as a boy, not the young man he'd become.

An old woman was bent over in prayer in the pew in front of me, holding her head in her hand. What was she praying for? I wondered. She seemed lost, somewhere far from this place, mumbling quietly to herself. I felt a strange connection with her; I, too, felt lost and far away. I thought about closing my eyes again in an attempt to conjure up a prayer, but the woman looked up momentarily and caught my gaze. Sensing that I was interrupting an intimate moment, I decided it was time to leave.

Walking out, I felt as though I'd been released from a dream. I looked left, the direction that the kind woman had indicated I should go, and briefly considered walking that way, but taking note of how low the sun was, I opted for the safety of retracing my steps and turned in the other direction. It might be better to stay in my comfort zone, for now. It had been a great day.

I hopped over the bronze sculpture on my way back to the hotel, feeling a new sense of consciousness, smiling all the way. So many new experiences. An awakening of my senses, perhaps. My perceptions.

8

STRIKE TWO

"Are you hungry?" Dennis asked. He'd returned to the hotel shortly after I had, earlier than expected.

I thought of all the wonderful eateries I'd passed that day—of all the smells and sights and sounds. It would be nice to share some of that with my husband.

"I'd love to go out to dinner! Then we could stroll along the canals. The city is like a fairy tale."

"Until you fall into one of the canals," he said, bluntly. "You'd come out a bag of bones. That water is filthy, full of germs."

"Wow, really?" I said, jarred back to the land of black and white but desperate to hold on to the momentum of the day that had offered me new, Technicolor memories. "I'd still love to go out on the town with you."

"I was planning on going downstairs to grab a bite in the

restaurant. I rarely leave the hotel on trips like this. Too risks. I can't afford to get sick. A merger is on the table, and that will require a whole other level of focus. But never mind that." He waved his hand dismissively. "You ready?"

As easy as that, we proceeded downstairs, and he ordered a burger with fries. I wanted to try the stamppot, a true Dutch meal: mashed potatoes, sauerkraut, carrots, onions, and kale served with a big juicy sausage. I was still salivating over memories of the wurst I'd eaten for lunch. But before I could place my order, Dennis did it for me—a burger and a salad. "Because you don't want those thighs to get too big and unruly."

He always chuckled after making these little comments, and I'd chuckle too, to keep the peace, but today I wasn't laughing. I wanted to get up and say, "No, I want the stamppot and that's what I'm going to get! You can get a salad instead of fries!" I wanted to stomp my foot and fold my arms across my chest. Of course, I did nothing of the sort. His ability to make me feel stupid, to silence me, had been perfected. I wondered if the server was checking to see how large my thighs actually were.

The meal was edible but nothing special. After all, hamburgers were American food, not Dutch. We ate mostly in silence in the almost-empty dining room. While everyone else in the city was eating delicious local food, here we were, the timid tourists, ordering American food in a foreign country. At one point Dennis asked about my day, but I hadn't even finished recounting my time at the flower market when he interrupted me.

"Don't count on me for dinner tomorrow. It's going to be a long day. Is three days in Amsterdam enough for you?" He snapped his fingers as he said this, signaling the server for the check.

"Oh, I'm just grateful to be here," I heard myself respond. Always the good wife.

"Here you go, Mr. Strum," said the server, placing the check and a pen in front of Dennis. "I hope everything was to your liking. Breakfast at the usual time?" He leaned forward as if waiting for an important piece of information.

"Yes, same time, and ask the chef to hold the sauce on my eggs." Dennis stood, and the server came over and pulled out my chair.

"I will let the chef know."

Dennis led the way out of the restaurant.

"You see how that server gave me extra attention? That's what a big tip gets you." He nodded as though thoroughly agreeing with himself and stepped into the elevator.

"Would you like to go for an after-dinner walk?" I asked, stepping in after him and praying he'd say yes.

"No, I'm looking forward to putting my feet up."

Despite it all, I just couldn't do it. I couldn't give up on being Dennis's wife. I wanted—needed him to see me, want me, love me. Especially now, after everything that had happened with our son.

My mother had once told me that I needed to try harder. And so, when the elevator door closed, I leaned into my husband and pressed myself against him. A tingling coursed up my body as my pelvic bone pressed into his leg. My hands went up to grasp the back of his neck. I could almost feel his lips against mine.

"What has gotten into you, Beth!" He jolted away from me. "We're in a public place. You know they have cameras in the elevators." He paused and looked up at the corners. "If you keep this up, I'll have to send you home early. Is that what you want? Are you ready to go home?"

"Of course not! I just wanted to thank you for a nice dinner."

"Well, if that's the case, the best thing you can do for me is let me put my feet up and rest."

It wasn't a physical strike. It never was. It wasn't even criticism or judgment. It was just plain honesty. He didn't have the desire to kiss me, hold me, love me. He didn't want to have anything to do with me. He wanted to be left alone. Why was I even here?

Many years ago, I'd resorted to talking to my mother about it, in a desperate attempt to gain perspective.

"Mom, is it natural to not have sex for years?"

She frowned a little. "What do you mean?"

"I mean that Dennis and I haven't had sex since our honeymoon, and our five-year anniversary is coming up."

"Well, some women would be glad to be rid of that drudgery." She smiled as though she spoke from experience, although I caught a glimpse of surprise in her eyes.

"Well, I'm not. I'm twenty-six years old and have had sex with my husband once in the past five years."

"Does he prefer other things?" she asked.

Like what? I wondered. *Other sexual things?* "No." He'd

never mentioned any desires he wanted to explore. Had never suggested things we could do. Explore. Nothing.

"Are you trying hard enough, Beth? Older men sometimes need a little help if you know what I mean?"

She spoke as if she were an expert, yet there hadn't been a man in her life since my dad took off.

"I *am* trying, Mom, but he's completely uninterested." I thought of the times when things hadn't work for Dennis—his disregard, his taking matters into his own hands, his refusal to give it another chance. To address it at all. It was as if he'd finished a tough chapter and had no desire to read on.

"Well, try harder," she said, a note of urgency creeping into her tone. "He's twenty years older than you, dear. You have to take that into account."

"He's forty-six, not seventy-six!" I blurted.

Still, she persisted. "Do you want to give up this life you have? The nice house? The nice friends? The nice cars? The best of everything?"

When I didn't answer, she continued. "Do you want to end up like—" She paused. "Alone?"

None of the things she'd listed fulfilled me. The only thing that fulfilled me was Troy. But when I considered my mother, without a man, raising me on her own . . .

It wasn't a life that I wanted to repeat.

"So what do you think I should do?" I finally asked.

"Find a way to make it work. Life isn't perfect. Be happy with what you have and don't be greedy." She sounded as if she were talking from a script, quoting some poem or movie.

I'd swallowed the words and let them settle uncomfortably in my stomach.

As the elevator door opened, I understood that I was holding out for a miracle. For Dennis to see me once again as the person he'd married, and for Troy to remember the first years of his life as being full of a mother's love. To remember that love was more important than money.

We lay on the bed in our hotel room, on top of the covers. Dennis turned down the TV a little and looked my way. "Did you find the reindeer yet?"

"No. I guess that will be on the top of my list for tomorrow. Do you have any idea where you bought it?"

He looked back at the TV with a sigh and turned it up to hear what the news anchor was saying about the US stock markets.

"Dennis?"

"Shhh, I'm trying to listen to this."

That night, I didn't sleep well. Melancholy clips of my life kept flickering in my mind, out of order: Dennis extending Troy's curfew even after we'd had a lengthy discussion about it. His refusal to back me when Troy didn't do his homework. When it came to Troy, when I said "white," Dennis would default to "black," eventually driving a huge wedge into my relationship with our son. And when it came to money, Troy had become like one of Pavlov's dogs, conditioned to salivate at the sight or mention of it. The more money, the more he salivated, already tasting the ease and privilege that his father's money would offer him.

How do I compete with that? Why should I have to compete with that?

I trembled with bitterness, an unfamiliar feeling. How had I let it get to this point? If I'd been more assertive, Troy would still be with us. That's what Dennis believed.

"This was your fault, Beth," he'd lament, whenever Troy came up in discussion. I wasn't a mind reader, but I was one-hundred-percent certain that what had happened couldn't be blamed on me alone.

Something about how all these feelings were surfacing felt dangerous. I felt as though I could end up doing something risky. Something I might not recover from.

9

Discovery

I'd slept in, but my last day in Amsterdam hadn't waited for me. As I readied myself to go out, I could hear the hum of cars below. Even though the city was filled with bikes and mopeds, there was an abundance of cars. Except in the pedestrian areas, of course. Exactly where I was headed.

The concierge gave me directions to a department store in the town center, where I'd begin my search for the porcelain reindeer. I was glad to have a mission. After everything that had come up the previous night, my mind needed something to latch on to.

At the center of the Old Town was a huge cobblestone square where street performers set up shop, hoping to receive enough donations in their caps or instrument cases to make a day's wages. How much would that be here? I wondered. Could a street performer really make a living posing as Marie Antoinette or Neptune and gesturing to their collection box only after a tourist had posed next to them for a photo?

From the center, streets jutted out in all directions like points of a star. I loved this design. It would make finding my way back from "getting lost" easier. The department store didn't have the reindeer, or any animals in the distinct blue-and-white style, for that matter, but I enjoyed wandering around in it. A clerk tried to sell me a porcelain replica of one of Amsterdam's churches, in which you could put a tea light. She had one illuminated on the counter.

"It is really lovely," I said, admiring it. "It reminds me of the old church I visited yesterday." Light flickered behind the tiny window openings.

"You mean Oude Kerk?"

"Yes, exactly!" I answered, tickled that I actually knew a landmark in the city.

"Well, then you must have it!" she said, smiling playfully.

"Actually, I was looking for something specific—a porcelain reindeer. One was given to me as a gift years ago, and I damaged it and want to replace it." I rummaged around in my purse and found a piece of it. "Here it is," I said, holding it up. "Do you carry this type of porcelain?" I asked, hoping perhaps I'd missed it while wandering the store.

She took the piece from me and examined it as though she were grading a diamond. It was then that I noticed how impeccably dressed she was, especially for a department-store clerk. She wore a long, narrow skirt, pantyhose, and a blouse covered by an open cardigan. Her pumps were coordinated with her skirt. *Who dresses like that anymore?* While I had worn a pair of nice wool pants and a sweater with my winter coat, she looked so much more put together. She reminded me of the actresses in the old Jimmy Stewart movies.

"Ah, I am sorry, we do not carry this line of porcelain, but I know a store that might. It is actually near the church you visited yesterday. I have seen this type of pottery there around the holidays. We Dutch are very specific about our porcelain," she said with a smile. "I am sure you have heard of delft. I can show you some fine pieces upstairs, or better yet, you can go to the town of Delft and have a great selection at your fingertips. It is only a few hours from here."

"Actually, this is my last day here."

"I see. You are American?"

"Yes, born and raised there."

"A big place, America. I have always wanted to visit, but it is very expensive to fly. I want to see New York City and Dallas and Hollywood."

I cleared my throat. "I've never been to any of those places."

She looked at me as though what I'd said was outlandish, reminding me of how sheltered a life I truly led.

"Would you like me to write down the address of the store for you?" She moved behind the counter to fetch a pad. "Or do you know the area well enough?"

"Oh, I'd love it if you could show me on this map." I pulled it out of my coat pocket. The paper was getting tender around the creases. That made me smile.

She spread it out on the counter. "It is not too far from

here, and it is not hard to find. It is off the main street, right here." She marked the path on the map with a blue pen.

"Is it in a pedestrian area?" I felt safer walking in places where I didn't have to watch for cars or traffic signals and signs that I couldn't read.

"Oh yes. In *the* pedestrian area." She smirked at me as if we were sharing a secret, except I wasn't privy to it. "And the church? Would you like me to wrap this up for you as well?" She cupped her hands around the illuminated church.

"Yes, I think this would be a perfect souvenir, especially if I don't find the reindeer."

"I agree. It is a very famous landmark." There was that smirk again.

Moments later, she handed me the package and gently slid the piece of broken reindeer back to me. "This is a perfect time to go," she said. "It gets crowded as evening approaches."

"Does everyone in Amsterdam do their shopping after work?"

"Something like that," she said, that grin lingering on her lips.

I easily found Sint Jansstraat, thanks to the path the salesclerk had drawn me. Dutch was so different from English. So many vowels and consonants strung together in unfamiliar orders. I was glad she hadn't tried to give me verbal directions—I would have ended up in the canal. As the tower of the Oude Kerk came into view, I knew I was heading in the right direction.

The wind had picked up, and the chill in the air, a stark

contrast to the cozy temperature of the store, made me button up my coat and squint. What I wouldn't give for a pair of boots like the ones I'd seen on the woman who'd given me a history lesson yesterday. *She* had been ready for the elements. I could also really use her angora hat right now. I pulled my scarf tight and brought up the collar of my coat to protect my face. Once I made the turn, the buildings on either side of me offered some protection. It was hard to believe that it could be so cold with the sun out among the fluffy clouds. When I looked up, those billowy clouds seemed to be moving across the sky with a sense of urgency, which spurred me on.

The charming facades of the buildings in the area served a dual purpose for me—their quaintness made me feel as if I were walking in a different time, long ago, and their height saved me from returning to the hotel to get warmer accessories.

The shop the salesclerk had recommended was called Les Petites Chattes, which was around the corner and one block from the church. I was pleasantly surprised to soon be standing in front of it. In its big navy-blue-trimmed window was a cat stretching itself out luxuriously among the vintage teapots and black velvet boxes that were open and placed strategically, displaying unique jewelry. The cat's tail flicked every so often, reminding window shoppers that this feline wasn't an inanimate part of the display.

Strands of holly wrapped with tiny lights framed the window, and a small Christmas tree decorated with a wide variety of ornaments stood in the center of it. On closer examination, I noticed that the ornaments were earrings, bracelets, and necklaces. Much to my glee, some familiar-looking blue-and-white porcelain animals had been placed around the tree, as if celebrating. I thought of my own window display and smiled. I didn't see a reindeer, but there were three ducks, two cats, and a fox. My hopes were high. One of the cats was curled up and the other was in the midst of a long stretch. I wondered what the cat in the window thought of the two renditions. Clearly, it couldn't be bothered with such trivial thoughts.

Ah, to be a cat.

When I entered, a string of bells on the door announced my arrival.

"Hoi," said a young woman, who appeared from behind a flimsy curtain hiding a wall of supplies.

"Hello."

"Oh, sorry. Hello. Not as many tourists come here in the winter. I know my shop is a bit off the beaten track. Can I help you with something?" On the counter was a big basket of pinecones, and she began decorating it with thick strands of gold and blue velvet ribbon. Noticing my gaze, she continued. "I am thinking of putting him in here, but I am not sure how." She picked up the teddy bear next to the basket that, by the look of him, had been very loved in a previous life. "This whole idea came to me when I found this little Saint Nicholas hat." She held up a blue hat accented with white fur and fit it on the bear.

"Oh, how cute! But why not a red hat, like Santa's?"

"You Americans," she answered playfully. "In the

Netherlands, we have St. Nicholas, and he wears blue and white. He also puts goodies in the shoes of children when they leave them on the stoop outside their front door, not under the Christmas tree."

"I see." I was stunned to learn that a color other than red represented Santa's suit, but I wasn't going to share my surprise. No need to further highlight my ignorance.

The cat had left the warmth of the window and jumped onto the counter. It rubbed its body against my coat. I reached out and returned the favor, petting the snuggly fur.

"You have made an impression on Sasha, our store mascot."

"Mascot?" I asked, confused.

"The name of the store is the Little Cats, in French. She is the last of the litter that was born in this store, years ago. She is quite a character." The shopkeeper smiled at the cat then shifted her attention back to her project.

"I was thinking of putting some shoes in this basket too, for a little holiday accent, but I cannot seem to make it work."

"What a clever idea." I loved her attention to detail. Along the edges of the floor were pairs of vintage shoes. "You have so many to choose from."

"Yes, I specialize in shoes and jewelry and teapots, but I sometimes carry specialty items during certain seasons. What can I help you find today?" She stopped threading the ribbons through the pinecones and wiped her hands on her apron.

I removed the piece of porcelain from my bag and held it up so she could see it.

"Oh dear, a holiday casualty." She peered at it. "Did you get this in my shop?"

"I'm not sure where it came from. My husband brought it back from a business trip in Amsterdam. I had a pair of them but this one broke, and I have to admit that I was the clumsy one."

There was that smirk again! Could this be a cultural characteristic? Or was I imagining things?

"I noticed that you have some animals in the window that look similar to my reindeer," I continued. "I was wondering if you have any in the back?"

She laughed and lifted up the curtain. "I am afraid that there is no back. The artist makes these animals specially for the holidays, and I usually sell out."

"Is there another store in the city where I could find them?"

"Oh no. I am the only store that carries them. She is a local artist who makes them as a hobby because she has a different full-time job. She has really made a name for herself and could probably sell them near the town center for a good deal more money, but she likes to support our community here, so she sells to me exclusively. We used to work together, years ago. The reindeer are always the first to sell out. Do you have the one that is lying down as well?"

"Yes, that one is still intact, but I'm in search of another standing one."

"And your husband told you where to find it?" she asked, with a touch of surprise in her voice.

I shook my head. "He said he couldn't remember where he got it."

"Of course." That smirk again. "Amsterdam is a big city." She went over to the window and picked up one of the ducks. "He is a handsome fella," she said, handing it to me for examination.

"He is cute, but I had my heart set on another reindeer. Do you think your artist will be making any more this season?"

"Hard to know, but you can always check back in a week or so. It depends how busy she gets with her clients. This is a hectic season." She returned the duck to its spot in the window. "Can I interest you in any jewelry or a pair of warm shoes?"

I glanced around, but my disappointment at not finding a replacement had left me without any further shopping inspiration.

"No, thank you. I wish I could check back in a week, but this is my last day in Amsterdam." As I uttered the words, a wave of sadness came over me. While not everything I'd been thinking and feeling over the last three days had been pleasant, at least I was feeling again, as though I'd had a numb limb that had started to tingle as blood flow returned to it.

"Well, make sure to sample some of our cheese. There is a shop on the corner that is very good and will give you samples."

"Thank you. I'm getting hungry. That's a perfect idea."

As I walked toward the door, the shop owner resumed her work on the basket of pinecones.

"Too bad I brought my lunch, or I would close up and join you," she said. "Make sure to try the smoked Gouda and the Edam cheese. Tell Tom that Maria from Les Petites Chattes sends her regards."

"I will. Thank you, Maria."

"And you never know, maybe your husband can buy you a reindeer next time he comes here on a business trip."

I'd already turned around, but I could sense that she was smirking again.

It unsettled me. What was I missing that everyone else was in on?

The minute I left the cozy shop, the cold breeze grabbed hold of me and had me walking quickly in the direction of the cheese shop. In the short time that I'd been inside, the sky had turned to a sheet of dark gray. It no longer held any promise of sunshine. Sasha, the cat, had been smart to soak it up while it lasted.

I entered the cheese shop carefully, as the entrance was filled with people waiting to make a purchase. It was a very popular place. Immediately I was intoxicated by the smells. There was cheese with truffles and cheese with lavender, cheese with caraway seeds and cheese with red waxy rinds—and each cheese could be sampled thanks to an ample supply of toothpicks and tiny squares in little blue-and-white bowls with labels.

Toward the back was a refrigerated section with pre-made sandwiches. I decided to go that route. It would be easier than trying to read and order from the menu on the wall. I bought one with smoked Gouda and roast beef with the intention of finding a bench out of the wind where I could eat, but to my disappointment, I couldn't find a single one. *How odd.* Then again, how would I survive on a bench outdoors in this frigid weather anyway? I was reminded of my naivety when it came to true winter weather. I wasn't in California anymore.

I opted to go back inside the cheese shop and share the only table, by the front window, with an older lady who was organizing her bag, packing the cheeses that she'd just purchased. I was grateful the store was busy. I'd be less conspicuous.

As I ate, I noticed wheels of cheese stacked in the shape of a Christmas tree in the window. Wait, I'd seen this shop before, on my first day in Amsterdam.

Was I in the Red Light District again? Or did all the cheese shops stack their wheels this way in honor of the season?

I looked out across the canal and indeed, there they were—the windows with women behind the glass. The street wasn't busy, unlike the last time I'd been here, so I had a clear view of the windows. One woman wearing tall, shiny boots and pink hot pants sat on a barstool, legs crossed. Instead of a shirt, suspender straps covered her nipples. She was preoccupied with her cell phone and looked bored, twirling a lock of her red hair with her free hand.

Next to her was a window with two women. One was blond and one had luminous, long brown hair that she draped forward over her breasts in lieu of a shirt. They talked to each other as if no one could see them in their negligees and garter belts. I was surprised to find that their lacey outfits looked like acceptable clothing—or was it the way they wore them that made me believe that?

I shouldn't be looking. It felt wrong. Yet I couldn't look away.

In another window, a woman was engaging with someone walking by. She opened her glass door and beckoned to a man in a suit. She said something in his ear as he got closer, and he smiled politely and shook his head before continuing on his way.

"Sorry, lady, this table is not for lookie-loos," said a man I'd seen behind the counter. He wiped his hands with a cloth as he approached. "I will have to ask you to leave."

I was about to laugh, but his expression conveyed that he was dead serious, borderline annoyed. Obviously, I'd deeply offended him. I felt my eyes fill with tears and quickly looked down and began to wrap up my sandwich. The store had emptied out, so the quiet made me feel even more uncomfortable and unwanted.

"I'm so sorry," I said, barely above a whisper. "I couldn't find a bench outside where I could sit." I was sure I sounded pathetic, but he softened a bit.

"Sitting outside in the winter is hardly an option in Amsterdam. To do that, you need to come back in June, July, and August. You must not be from around here."

"No, I'm from California."

"No wonder," he said with a snicker. He gestured to the table. "Why don't you finish your sandwich before you go about your day. It is my fault anyway—I need to remove this table. Too many people want to stand around and gawk. They have no respect. Like those boys over there." He pointed across the canal. "Do you know what they are doing?"

I looked over and saw six guys around Troy's age huddled together, talking and laughing and passing money to each other.

I frowned. "No, what are they doing?"

"They are pooling their money so one of them can get lucky." He wiped the table I'd been standing at. "It is how they go about doing it that is so disrespectful."

I shook my head, speechless. I didn't understand his line of thinking. Wasn't that what these women wanted? Wasn't that what this place was all about? Nothing like this would be allowed to exist, in plain sight in the light of day, in America, except, perhaps, in the Westerns, in the old saloons. And that was Hollywood, not reality. I found his concern for the prostitutes unsettling.

"Oh boy, Miriam is up to some street cleaning again." The man chuckled, still looking out the window. He seemed distracted by the scene, hands on his hips and shaking his head with a smile. I took the opportunity to slip out before he noticed, having not quite recovered from my embarrassment.

Walking over the canal bridge, back to the hotel, I paused at the crest and watched as a woman made her way toward the group of guys with a broom. She walked with a sense of determination, navigating the cobblestones flawlessly in her heels. She wore a tiny skirt, and her short, tight sweater with a low scoop offered a clear view of her ample cleavage.

"Move along boys," she said. "Got to get the garbage off the street." She feigned sweeping the sidewalk where they were standing. There wasn't a spot of trash in sight. "Come on, move along." They quickly made their way down the cobblestone walkway, seemingly put off by her directness.

"Hoi, Miriam." I glanced back to see the cheese man waving at the woman with the broom.

She looked over and smiled. "Hoi, Tom." She raised her broom in a wave.

As I crested the bridge, I paused and looked in the empty window that she had walked back towards.

The woman reached for the knob and opened the glass door but before she closed it, she glanced back at me and I realized that I'd been staring, frozen in my tracks on the cobblestones, watching this colorful exchange.

There was something familiar about her. Something I couldn't put my finger on. Of course, I wouldn't know anyone in this part of town. How preposterous! And yet, my feet wouldn't move. It was as if unknown forces were controlling me.

"You are on the wrong street, darling," she remarked, as she tipped her head to the left, giving me a direction for my exit.

I blinked. That voice. That accent. I suddenly recognized it. It was the voice of the beautiful woman who'd stopped to talk to me yesterday. The one with the flowers in her arms. The one who'd been impeccably dressed. The smart one who'd encouraged me to go into the Oude Kerk, after giving me a bit of a history lesson. There was no doubt about it.

That woman was a prostitute.

10

JUDGMENT

It started to snow as I made my way back to the hotel. I felt as if I were in a trance, unable to process what I'd just witnessed. How could that be the same woman? She'd been so refined when I met her, during her routine of buying flowers and spreading beauty around . . . to where? Other women in the windows? Her customers? I had envied her, wanted to be like her, judged her by the impression she'd made on me. She'd been so kind, so knowledgeable. I couldn't wrap my head around it.

The silent snow stuck on my sleeves. How beautiful it was, as it began to cover everything from bare branches to windowsills with a fine layer of what looked like spun sugar. Lights began to flicker on in shops, and the yellow glow offered a feeling of coziness, despite the frigid temperature.

What a day.

I checked my watch—4:00 p.m. Just enough time for a hot bath before dinner.

Soon, I was dropping myself down under the thick pile of bubbles in the bathtub of our hotel room. The warm water instantly relaxed me, and the bubbles gave me a place to hide. I deeply inhaled the scent of lavender. I never took baths anymore. One time, early in our marriage, Dennis had walked in on me while I was taking a bath and recoiled as if he'd found me participating in some lewd act.

"My god, Beth. What are you doing?"

His words had left my heart covered with welts. *What's wrong with taking a bath?* But that was all it had taken. After that, I limited myself to showers. I found myself changing anything that Dennis criticized without question. And he criticized a lot.

Now, immersed in the biggest bubble bath I'd ever taken, I felt giddy. My knees stuck out of the bubbles like two brown mountain peaks peering through the clouds. I coated my arms and knees, piling the bubbles on in layers so that all that was visible was my head, sticking out of the water like a spirit.

Giggling, I made silly hats and facial hair—something I'd done with Troy when he was young. He'd loved when I made tall pointy cones of bubbles on his head and long pointy beards of bubbles on his chin. We'd talk in funny voices, creating accents for each bubble person.

As the bubbles began to dissipate, I instantly became uncomfortable in the revealing water. I couldn't remember the last time I'd looked at myself in the mirror—I mean really looked at myself. My reflection had become something that I avoided at all costs. I thought of the women I'd seen that afternoon, of how brazen they were to show so much of themselves. And yet there they were, window after window, posing with such disregard for how people viewed them.

Stepping out of the bathtub, I wrapped a towel around my head and then reached for the fluffy white robe on the back of the door. As I stood in front of the big, lit-up mirror, curiosity overcame me. What did I look like naked these days?

Letting my hands drop, I slowly opened the robe, exposing a light-brown swatch of skin. The bodies I'd seen in the windows varied in shape and size, but all the women had appeared confident. That confidence likely made them more desirable. It was a characteristic I lacked. But what if I'd been underestimating how attractive I was?

I answered my question without any help. If I were attractive, my husband would want me. I wouldn't lose a little more dignity every time I attempted to reach out to him.

I stood there, motionless, daring myself to open my robe. Then I pulled it tightly around me and left the bathroom to get dressed.

Feeling a fresh burst of timidity after my moment in front of the mirror, I went downstairs to the hotel restaurant to eat dinner. It saddened me, how quickly I'd reverted, but it didn't surprise me.

The waiter seemed prepared to receive me. He, too, was well practiced in his ways.

"Good evening, Mrs. Strum. Your husband told me you'd be coming for dinner. Would you like to sit in his spot?" He waited for my response as though he were waiting for air. How could I say no?

"Of course. That would be perfect."

It wasn't perfect. It was in a quiet corner, out of view of most of the restaurant. I couldn't even people-watch.

"Would you like a menu, or will you be having the same as last night?" He leaned in again, waiting patiently, and I half expected him to laugh. He didn't.

"Actually, I'd like the stamppot, please." At least I could order what I wanted tonight.

"Excellent. Mr. Strum likes to stick with his favorite, but I'll be happy to put that order in. Would you like something to drink?"

"Yes, a glass of white wine."

"Right away, Mrs. Strum."

He walked away with purpose in his step, and when my dinner arrived, I almost invited him to sit with me, since the restaurant was mostly empty. The stamppot was delicious. How could Dennis bear eating so many burgers in Amsterdam? Did he eat hotel burgers in Germany and France too?

Dennis rolled in at eight thirty and was unusually chipper.

"So did you find the reindeer?" he asked, settling himself back on his pillows and working his socks off with his toes.

I turned onto my side to face him on the bed and placed

my head in my hand. "No, but I did find the store that carried it."

That seemed to get his attention. "Only one store carries those decorations? That seems hard to believe."

"I showed a salesclerk at a department store a piece of the reindeer, and she recognized the porcelain right away and told me where I could find it."

"I see. But you didn't get one?"

I tried not to show my confusion. His curiosity was odd.

"No, they didn't have any reindeer. She tried to sell me a duck and a cat made by the same artist, but I wanted to replace the broken reindeer." I paused. "And you'll never believe where I ended up after that," I said, wanting to take advantage of his sudden interest and actually engage him in a conversation about my day.

"Where?"

"The Red Light District! I even watched one of the women shoo away some young guys with a broom."

He turned to look at me so fast that I startled. My head fell to my pillow.

"You have an entire city to explore, and you go to the dirtiest part? What's wrong with you?"

I quickly sat up. "I didn't mean to. The store with the porcelain was just around the corner."

"Oh, like I'm supposed to believe that? Nobody ends up in the Red Light District by accident." He looked at me with disgust. "I can't believe you'd go there."

"Dennis," I said, feeling panic rise in my chest, "I told you I didn't realize where I was." He never took me places, and now that he had, I'd disappointed him. He'd never invite me on another trip. "Have you ever been there?" I asked, hoping to salvage the conversation.

"Of course not! Why would I go there? You should be ashamed of yourself. The city has museums, parks, stores . . ." He shook his head. "And you go to the bowels of this place. It's a good thing we're leaving tomorrow because if we weren't, I'd be buying you a ticket home, right now."

I fell silent. No need to ask him if he'd bought the reindeer at Les Petites Chattes. Obviously, the answer was no.

The car picked us up at nine o'clock on Wednesday morning to take us to Rotterdam, international headquarters for West Tech Systems and the city where Dennis and I would spend the rest of the trip. The snow had stopped sometime overnight and most of it had melted, but the gray sky remained. It was synonymous with my spirits.

Despite the dressing-down I'd received the night before, I didn't want to leave Amsterdam. Beyond sightseeing opportunities, the city had offered me a long-awaited reunion with my old self. A peek at the old me. I'd felt more willing to think and act independently when I was alone, and this freedom had felt so good.

So necessary.

"Your first time in Amsterdam, Mrs. Strum?" the driver asked, eyeing me in the rearview mirror.

"Yes," I replied hesitantly, not sure if I should elaborate or if that would bother Dennis. He was absorbed in his laptop.

"And your impressions?

"I loved it," I said with a grin. "I went to the Van Gogh Museum, the ice-skating rink, the Christmas market. Oh, and I tried to buy tulips at the flower market and found out that they confiscate them at the airport!"

I noticed that Dennis had stopped typing and was looking at me with raised eyebrows, as if this was all news to him. Maybe it was. It seemed he only paid attention when I said something he didn't want to hear. Was he waiting for me to mention where I went yesterday? I'd certainly never talk about that again.

"And how long are you staying in Rotterdam, Mr. Strum?" the driver asked politely.

"About a week, I believe," Dennis said, looking at his laptop again. "There are some big things happening as we approach the end of the year."

"WTS is making its mark here in Holland," the driver said with a nod. Apparently, he knew more than I did about the company.

My interest in the business had ended early on in our marriage, after Dennis told me not to badger him with questions when he got home. *It's not necessary to know what's going on at WTS*, I'd told myself. My place was in the home, caring for Troy and making appearances as a loving wife when needed. I'd done my job well. At least I'd thought so until recently.

"And how are the wife and kids?" Dennis asked the driver.

My husband also played his role well. He had a knack

for making people feel good when he wanted to. I hadn't been among those people for a long time.

"Good, thank you, sir. My wife is busy with the kids. Our youngest is proving to be strong-willed and keeps her on her toes." The driver chuckled. "And how is your son?"

Out of the corner of my eye, I saw Dennis tense up slightly, but his voice remained calm and steady. "Good. He's a very busy young man. Always on the go."

"Still playing soccer?"

"No, he had to step away from it to focus on his academics. He's preparing for his college entrance exams now."

Dennis kept his eyes on his laptop screen, but I was certain he could sense my shock.

All blatant lies! What on earth had he told the driver?

"How is that girlfriend of his? Is she still doting on him?" The driver looked up at the rearview mirror again, trying to catch Dennis's eye.

Dennis chuckled and met the man's gaze briefly. "You know those girls. When they find a good catch, they jump on it, isn't that right, Beth?"

He glanced at me with a look of warning in his expression.

What I wanted to say was "What the hell are you talking about?" What I offered was a weak "Uh-huh."

Here I was, a world away from our son, beating back the ache in my chest. Right now, seeing and talking to him was impossible. What was equally impossible was the picture that Dennis had painted of him. Was that the person he wished Troy were? Did he just tell people about his ideal version of his son? I knew nothing about a girlfriend!

I recalled some famous lines from *As You Like It*, which I'd read in junior college: *"All the world's a stage, and all the men and women merely players."* The professor had spent weeks on Shakespeare, and I'd kept a notebook full of quotes that seemed timeless in nature. *"They have their exits and their entrances; and one man in his time plays many parts."*

Had I missed an act in the play that was our life?

The driver took the next exit and pulled off the freeway, and less than an hour later we were driving down a smaller expressway surrounded by towering modern buildings. I peered out of the window. This city was nothing like Amsterdam. It looked more like pictures I'd seen of Chicago and New York. But what did I know? Of course the Netherlands would have its modern parts too. I'd fallen in love with the Old Town of Amsterdam, though—all the bricks and bridges, the cobblestones and canals, the church steeples and domes. It had lived up to my expectations of a European city. Rotterdam was all high-rises, and everything seemed to be made of chrome and steel and glass.

Some of the structures looked like works of art, almost as if the architects had been competing to create the most unusual buildings. There was a building in the shape of a periscope, and one that looked like six rectangular boxes stacked in a way that suggested the building would tip over. There was a modern arch spotted with windows, and hexagonal glass domes.

As we drove along the river, I saw a sign that identified

its name: *Nieuwe Maas*. Ahead was a bridge held up with strong iron cables. It was much wider than those quaint little bridges I'd walked over fifteen hours ago.

"Wow, that's a lot of water," I said, mostly to myself. I caught Dennis looking at me, and he shook his head as if to say, "Please don't embarrass me with your stupid comments."

But the driver, obviously proud of the city, eagerly said, "Oh, that's the Nieuwe Maas River, or the New Maas River. It's a northern tributary of the Rhine. Have you heard of the Rhine? Most Americans know about it but know very little about the Maas."

"Oh yes," I said, to avoid further humiliation. I hadn't known about either river.

"The Maas is a very important river. It connects Rotterdam to the North Sea. Our city's nickname is the Gateway to Europe because of this river system."

"That's so interesting," I said, as the car slowed in the traffic. "Everything here looks so modern compared to Amsterdam."

"Well, Amsterdam has its modern section as well, but your hotel was located in the heart of the Old Town, and every tourist loves the Old Town. We Dutch like the new stuff and you Americans like the old stuff." He chuckled. "You see, Rotterdam's city center was destroyed in World War II. Many feel like these new buildings are the pride and joy of our city."

That made sense. I couldn't imagine living somewhere that had once been ruined by war. And I had to admit that the city was beautiful. It just wasn't what I wanted to see.

I longed for the sausage stand and the pedestrian walking areas, not this city with multi-lane traffic and hurried, impersonal energy. I didn't say any of this. I was sure I'd already said too much for Dennis's liking.

Soon, we pulled up to a tall building with shiny steel accents and a triangular roof. Across the street was a building whose roof was also triangular but at a slanted angle. It made me think of a spaceship. Perhaps it had just landed here among all the steel and glass. The building appeared to be a hive of activity. People dashed in and out of it.

"What is that?" I asked.

"Are you referring to your hotel or the train station?" the driver asked. "The tall one is your hotel, and the train station is across the street. The station is another source of pride and joy for our city." He beamed. "You can take the train all over the country, and to Brussels and Paris as well."

I brightened. "To Amsterdam?"

"As fast as thirty-one minutes!"

The driver stopped the car and hopped out to get the door for us, and I followed Dennis to the monolith. Various flags welcomed us into the five-star hotel. I guessed that meant it was international? I gaped as we entered the massive lobby. It looked as if it could have offered refuge to all the residents of Sand City. Everywhere I turned there was glass, and on the other side of that glass was a world of high-rises and busy people and traffic. I felt an odd desire to see a solid wall—something to protect me from the hustle and bustle.

Anxiety crept up. Had I left all my sense of adventure back in Amsterdam?

Thankfully, we were soon in our room on the seventh floor. Dennis was a preferred customer, so we hadn't had to stand in line or even touch our luggage. I know this meant a lot to Dennis, but I had no trouble negotiating my own luggage, if need be. While three of the walls were solid, the fourth was entirely glass and offered an extensive view of Rotterdam. It leaned out between the floor and the ceiling at a forty-five-degree angle. Though a great architectural feat, it left me even more unsettled. It seemed as though I could fall through the glass, to my death, if I got too close. I hated the feeling but wasn't sure what I hated more: being in this new, modern hotel with angled windows for walls or being away from the familiarity of Amsterdam.

I sat down shakily on the bed as Dennis moved to the window to gaze out. "This will do," he said, as if surveying his kingdom.

11

STUCK

For the next couple of days, I worked on perfecting the art of distraction. I read my book, exercised in the hotel's extensive gym, and used the sauna, where I was the only woman that wore a swimsuit. I played game after game of sudoku.

But I couldn't totally distract myself from thinking about the lies that Dennis had told the driver.

I didn't have the nerve to broach the subject. My husband would surely have a perfectly rational reason for the untruths and, once again, I'd feel like an idiot for even bringing them up.

By Thursday evening, I'd come to appreciate the clarity the exercise was giving me. I'd loved running and doing ab workouts before I got married, but Dennis had asked me to stop running since it would take me away from the house. I liked to drive down to the beach or along the rec path near Monterey, but Dennis felt it was a waste of time and my place was at home if Troy needed me. So I quit running. Just as I'd stopped doing so many other things. *Why had I let him dictate how I should live?* I'd kept up my ab work, though, and had a toned tummy as proof that I'd kept something for myself. Not that I ever received any appreciation from my husband regarding my commitment to staying fit. That usually came from Dennis's coworkers at work functions, who also happened to call Dennis "the best thing that ever happened to me." I was only now starting to have serious doubts about that.

While running on the treadmill in the hotel gym earlier that day, a thought had struck me: *I'm a mere requirement in my husband's life.* I allowed him to avoid the harassment that came with being single.

How had I never seen this? How had I become so unaware? Had I ever had awareness? More importantly, could I continue this way, now that I'd seen a sliver of a bigger world? I felt a strange sense of rebellion as I ran on the treadmill. It didn't take me out of the room, but it took me out of my feeble mind that had been wasting away and that was helping me understand what I had given up in this marriage.

"What did you do today?" Dennis asked, when he returned to the room. He didn't seem to care that I wasn't leaving the hotel. Though his indifference made me bristle, I was glad that he wasn't pushing me to go out—I simply had no desire to rush around among the humanity sprawled across the cement seven stories down, nor did I want to dodge the cars and buses racing to their destinations. I was content to pass the time indoors, where no one could bother me and I could avoid ending up in the wrong part of town.

Just as we had in Amsterdam, we ate our meals in the hotel, and I began to see yet another side to Dennis. What I'd always thought was worldliness was beginning to look a lot like ignorance. His work was his world, and when he wasn't doing it, he shut down, like a computer. Rather, he pressed a pause button, and I was part of that pause. He was a master at his job and a failure at his personal life. I had let that failure become an integral part of my existence. I was beginning to see the threads that held my weary life together. They were loosening. There wasn't much uniting our lives in a partnership.

These revelations fueled my workouts. I challenged myself to run faster on the treadmill and added power boosts to my spin-bike workouts. I also tried out the elliptical and rowing machines. The equipment had evolved since I'd last worked out in a gym, and I was eager to try it all. I worked with the free weights and the resistance bands until my arms felt like jelly and my legs rubber. I loved every minute of it. The exercise helped me remember the personal power I'd let slip away. Exercise was one thing I could hold on to, one part of the Old Beth that was being recovered. What else might I be able to excavate from the wreckage?

Friday after work, Dennis returned to the room and announced,

"The team here is hosting a dinner party for me tomorrow and requested that you attend. What do you think?

Would you like to get out and see how the rich and famous of Rotterdam live?" He smiled a Cheshire-cat smile, so pleased with himself for being part of this small circle of successful people. I knew this wasn't a question. I'd never be allowed to turn down an opportunity for him to have his ego stroked.

"Where will it be?" I asked, wondering if some bigwig was offering up his house, as Dennis did on occasion—leaving all the planning to me, of course.

"A restaurant near the center of Rotterdam. It's a favorite of many. Dress up." He walked toward the bathroom, signaling an end to the conversation. "It may be your only chance."

Even though it was Saturday, Dennis had to work, so I took my time getting ready, after a rigorous workout. I wanted my body stripped of any tension so that there'd be plenty of room for the new tensions I was sure would accumulate. My days of working out were already evident, and I allowed myself the luxury of feeling good in my little black dress as I fastened my pearls, a gift from Dennis early in our marriage.

The phone in the hotel room rang, taking me by surprise. "Hello?"

"Beth, things ran late at work. I'm going to send a car for you. Go downstairs in ten minutes and it should be waiting."

"How will I know which car?" I asked, my inexperience shining through.

"Ask the valet. You know who that is, right?"

His condescending remark didn't set a positive tone for the evening, but what had I expected?

As promised, a car was waiting for me when I stepped outside the hotel for the first time since arriving, days ago. "Where to?" the driver asked, although I was sure he'd already been informed by Dennis and was just being polite.

I said the name of the restaurant carefully, wanting to get it right.

"A local favorite. You will be treated to the best in Rotterdam. You must try the eel."

I held my tongue. I had no intention of trying the eel, or any other odd delicacy. All I wanted was to get through the evening without criticism. I didn't want to hear about how I'd talked too much, or too little, about how I hadn't circulated or used good-enough vocabulary.

"May I say, you look beautiful, this evening, miss?" the driver said with a smile, glancing in his rearview mirror.

I gratefully accepted the compliment. It had been a long time since I'd received one.

"Have you seen much of the city during your stay?" he continued.

"Not really."

"You should get out and see what the city has to offer."

"Yes, I really should." I agreed with him, one-hundred-percent, but as we headed toward the city center, I saw nothing that enticed me. How had I become so small-minded?

Tomorrow, I'll go out and about, I promised myself. I'd give Rotterdam a try. I wouldn't be the American who went to the Netherlands and ordered hamburgers.

"You are in a perfect location to take advantage of the train station across the street. You could visit many of our beautiful cities. Gouda is not far away, and neither is Delft, which is a lovely representation of old, traditional Holland. It depends on whether you want cheese or china—or maybe both!" The driver looked in his rearview mirror again. I gave a nod, feeling suddenly overwhelmed. "Leiden is a wonderful college town," he continued, "and then there's always Amsterdam, but I believe your husband said that you were already there. You probably want to see something new."

I nodded again. But I would have given anything to be back in Amsterdam.

Minutes later, the driver parked and opened my door. I tried to adopt an air of intelligence and sophistication as I headed to the entrance of the restaurant. He quickly moved ahead of me and opened the door. "Have a wonderful evening, madam."

"Thank you. You too."

The restaurant was long and narrow and offered little chance of not spotting someone. The bar was toward the front, and I immediately recognized Dennis standing at it. His back was to me, and I didn't recognize the woman next to him. She was older and not conventionally beautiful, but she stood so close to him it took my breath away.

Feeling paralyzed, I stopped and watched them. She leaned against his arm with ease. Not even in sleep was I offered the luxury of close touch like that. They were laughing about something, and she laid her hand lightly on his shoulder. He placed his hand on the small of her back. She then took her glass of wine and walked to the back of the room, where the dinner party was gathering.

Stirring myself, I came up behind Dennis and leaned into him just as she had, praying for the same response. He turned slowly, as though drinking up the contact, and then his eyes landed on me. He didn't lose his smile, but I felt him tense up.

"Oh, there you are," he said, creating a little space between us. "I was beginning to worry that you weren't going to show."

"Really?" I replied, trying to suppress my annoyance. "Did you really think I'd do that to you?"

"Nah, I know you like it when you get to be a part of my world," he said with a smirk, and pushed a few bills across the bar. He pointed to the bartender and winked. The bartender responded with a look that hinted he wasn't impressed by my husband's pretentious show of excessive tipping.

Had I really never noticed his arrogance before?

The evening rolled out slowly. I was introduced to Dennis's Dutch colleagues, including Lydia, the woman I'd seen on his arm when I walked in. She'd worked with the company for twenty-one years and was a widow with two older children and several rabbits. I soon learned that rabbits were a common pet in the Netherlands. Lydia seemed nice, and under other circumstances, I wouldn't have given her a second thought. She even went out of her way to make sure I was comfortable, coming to stand beside me when I had no one to talk to. I knew the exchange I'd witnessed at the bar had been benign, but I hungered for intimacy. My husband didn't even want to kiss me in an empty elevator.

At one point, a man named Eric, whom I'd been introduced to earlier in the evening, came up behind Dennis and gave him a big pat on the back.

"How was your visit to Amsterdam today?" Eric said, taking a swig of his drink. "Was it busy for a Saturday? I try to avoid it on the weekend." He smiled and moved on to another group of people, not waiting for an answer.

I blinked and looked at Dennis. "You went to Amsterdam today?" I asked, stunned. Why would he go there alone? He was working at the headquarters in Rotterdam now. Why wouldn't he tell me?

"Eric must have confused me with someone else," Dennis replied with a shrug. "I didn't go to Amsterdam. Three days was enough for me."

"Oh."

"Let me refresh your drink," Dennis offered. Before I could respond, he grabbed my half-full glass of white wine and headed for the bar. Several of Dennis's male colleagues eyed me with approval as I waited for Dennis to return, and it brought me a little relief to know that someone could see the efforts I put into being Mrs. Strum.

All evening, Dennis was his charming self, tossing compliments and claiming humility. It was his secret to success in this world of business: "Make people feel good and make yourself appear less commanding than you actually are." I had to give him credit for how he'd navigated his career; it was his personal life that needed some direction. Even while we stood next to each other, I never once felt his hand on my back or his breath in my ear.

That night, I had a hard time going to sleep. I kept thinking about how at ease Dennis had been with Lydia and about how I wouldn't have witnessed these shows of affection if I hadn't arrived at the restaurant when I did. In my eyes, it was a betrayal.

When I finally went to sleep, I dreamed of Dennis surrounded by ladies fanning him with fronds. They stroked him with their hands, and he smiled in the same way that he had with Lydia. He was propped up on a lounge chair next to a long, elaborate indoor pool. The air felt tropical. Palm trees stood in every corner.

In the dream, I walked in and he dismissed all the women with the snap of his fingers, leaving us in a cold, empty room.

12

The Shift

I woke up with resolve. I was getting out of this hotel. My world was becoming too small, and I needed some perspective. I could tell by the movement of the trees down below that it was windy, yet I had no idea if it was cold or warm, sealed up in the room of glass as I was.

Dennis had informed me the previous night that he'd be working through the weekend and I'd be on my own. This information had given me the burst of courage I'd needed. I'd go forth beyond the walls of the grand hotel.

Once dressed and in the lobby, I was faced with a dilemma: Where to go? The concierge had his hands full with a large family who wanted to see everything in one day, so I stepped outside and gazed around. Across the street stood the train station that reminded me of an extraterrestrial vessel. Maybe I could start there.

I made my way to the station via the bike tunnel that went under the busy street, and as soon as I stepped into the building, I was struck by how much it seemed like a museum. I much preferred the central station in Amsterdam, which was dark and made of brick. It made me believe that I'd stumble upon Platform Nine and Three-Quarters and would soon see Harry Potter and his friends come out of the wall. Still, this building was magnificent. I peered up at the roof of wood and glass which gave the interesting illusion that it was folded. How many people even took the time to really look at this place?

Around me, people moved with purpose, heading out for an adventure, heading home, heading to lunch appointments or weekend visits. Where was I going?

I studied the departures board and noted all the places one could go: Delft, Gouda, Antwerp, Maastricht, even Paris and London. But the destination that jumped out to me was Amsterdam.

I approached a man at the service counter, and he informed me that there were 102 trains to Amsterdam per day, the cost was sixteen euros, and the duration was about forty-four minutes.

My jaw dropped. I could be in Amsterdam in less than an hour and for less than twenty US dollars. There was a train leaving in fourteen minutes.

Would it be a big mistake? Maybe I'd get kidnapped? I hadn't even left a note for Dennis.

To hell with it!

With the help of a kind local, I soon found myself seated

on a train bound for Amsterdam. And I felt as though I finally understood the phrase "flying by the seat of your pants."

Something had happened to me, slowly but surely, over the last few days. Was this the tipping point that people talked about?

The doors closed, an announcement was made in Dutch, and the train lurched forward. I was on my way.

"Is this your first visit to Amsterdam?" the old man seated next to me inquired.

"No," I said, disappointed to be giving the impression that I was a novice. "I've been there before."

"Have you been to Anne Frank's house? Every American goes there."

"It's actually not on my list."

"Well, that's a surprise." He looked at me and smiled. "There is so much more to our city than Anne Frank's house. I get annoyed when I see the long lines of people wanting a glimpse of a house from our dark past while the beauty of Amsterdam goes unnoticed."

"I can see your point," I said, but he wasn't finished.

"People love to keep the bad memories alive. What would happen if we just let them go?"

Feeling self-conscious, I glanced around to see if anyone was listening to this conversation, but no one seemed to be interested in my interaction with this seemingly eccentric old man.

"Perhaps people think that if we forget about history, we may repeat our mistakes," I said.

"How has that worked out so far? If that were true, why

are we still making the same mistakes over and over?" He grinned and shook his finger playfully. "That's what you get when you sit by an old man: truth and a little bit of wisdom."

While his comments were generalizations, I felt like he was talking about my life: the way I let myself become a servant to Dennis and let go of all that made me Beth. Over and over and over again. It made me unsettled.

"Thank you," I said with a small smile, shifting toward the window, but he still wasn't done with me. From his pocket he removed a handkerchief bearing three stripes: red, white, and blue.

"Let's test your knowledge of the Netherlands," he said, holding up the handkerchief. "I know your American flag is red, white, and blue, but you have stars and stripes, and we only have stripes, as do the French. Both of these European flags have the same three colors, but one has horizontal stripes, and one has vertical stripes."

I nodded politely.

"So, which is the Dutch flag? This way?" He held the handkerchief so that the stripes ran vertically. "Or this way?" He turned it so the stripes were horizontal.

"I have no idea. Can you give me a hint?" I didn't want to waste his time with my ignorance, but he seemed to be having fun.

"OK, I will teach you the trick my father taught me when I was very little so I could remember which flag was which. The Netherlands has always battled with the sea. It keeps trying to steal land from our little country, so we Dutch have been forced to build dikes and canals. Since water is the basis of the country's struggle, you will find it at the base of the Dutch flag." He turned his handkerchief so that the stripes were horizontal and the blue one was at the bottom.

He turned it again, so the stripes were vertical. "This is the French flag. If you ask me, the French have made it very difficult for foreigners to distinguish between the two. I have no idea what their flag represents. Every time I have asked a French person, I have gotten a different story. One person told me it represents the French Revolution. Another said it represented freedom. Another said it represented the clergy and the nobility. They need to get their story straight. Our flag came first, in the seventeenth century. Now you will not have any trouble identifying it."

"And what do the colors on the Dutch flag mean?" I asked, genuinely interested now.

"Red stands for the people—we are at the top. White stands for the church and blue for nobility." He smiled with a sense of pride. It was a smile I'd seen on others in the country. "But you will rarely see people flying the Dutch flag outside their homes like you Americans. We leave the flag-flying to the government."

The man then blew his nose into the handkerchief, making a honking sound, before putting it back in his jacket pocket.

I chuckled, and we remained silent for the rest of the trip. I appreciated the man's honesty, an attribute that seemed common among the Dutch. The woman who'd helped me navigate the train station and purchase the right ticket had

had a similar demeanor, and the Dutch men I'd talked to at the business dinner the night before had been straightforward and pragmatic. This was all new to me. I much preferred their matter-of-fact way of discussing things to words steeped in innuendos and double meanings. That was my husband's language.

Thanks to Dennis, I guess I'm bilingual, I thought wryly.

After disembarking in Amsterdam, I took a minute to get my bearings in the dark station. I once again felt as though I'd stepped back in time. I grinned. No sign of Harry Potter and his friends, though.

At street level, I was pleased to find I knew exactly where I was. I walked to the entrance of the hotel we'd stayed in, which was only two blocks away and easy to spot due to the many poles bearing waving flags. I thought about how my husband had ordered us a taxi to take us from the train station to the hotel when we first arrived in the city. Two blocks. We could have walked!

Since it was almost noon, I decided to head to the Christmas market to get a sausage. All this newfound excitement was making me hungry. The line was long but well worth the wait again. From there, I returned to the flower market to surround myself with beauty. I wanted to play it safe for now, visiting places I already knew.

The flower market was a lot busier than it had been the last time I visited, so I ducked into a nearby linen shop to admire the fabrics. I'd never learned to sew, but growing up, I had a friend whose mother made her dresses. I'd always wanted one of these homemade items, but sewing required money, so this hobby was never a consideration. Now, looking at the selection of fabrics and textures, I fantasized about the kinds of skirts and dresses that would suit the materials. *What a fun store to work in!* I thought. I was sure anyone who applied would need to be a good seamstress. I just liked the fabrics.

When the crowd in the flower market appeared to have thinned a little, I returned and was soon admiring a grand assortment. I couldn't believe these flowers could blossom in the frigid Dutch winter.

"Hoi, Miriam," the flower vendor called out.

"Hoi, Albert."

I whirled around to look, recognizing the voice, the unique accent—and the name. There she was, the woman who'd talked to me near the church and who'd shooed away the loitering boys.

She and the vendor had a conversation in Dutch punctuated by laughter. Her accent was a little different than his but maybe she came from a different area in Holland just like southerners in the United States. I moved toward the checkout counter, feigning interest in the red-and-white amaryllis bulbs and blooms close to her, so that I could get a better look. She had on the same angora hat but instead of her long coat, she wore a brilliant magenta wool jacket that drew attention to her dark-brown hair, which rested flawlessly on her shoulders. Her plaid scarf also contained threads of magenta. The combination was perfect. She wore a narrow black wool skirt with black boots. Different boots this time. I couldn't help but gape. She looked as if she'd just stepped out of her own private dressing room and was ready for a photo shoot.

As the vendor wrapped her flowers, I wondered if he knew where she worked. Did she lead a double life? Did she work in the Red Light District and also have a husband and family? Could that be possible? Could he be one of *her* customers?

When she left, I thought I saw her glance my way, but she walked on without a word, her sharp heels clicking on the cobblestones, marking a confidence I longed to feel. I had an urge to follow her. I wanted to know her path, her story, her life. Was she heading to the Red Light District now? Dennis had said that this was the most undesirable place in Amsterdam, and that I had no business there, but he wasn't here . . .

I decided to give her a head start and then make my way to the Oude Kerk to see for myself if she could bring beauty to a place known for ugly immorality. I'd have to keep my eye on the time, to make sure I got back to Rotterdam at a decent hour. I'd circled a few options on the schedule while en route.

What would Dennis think if he knew where I was?

Today, I would choose to not care. My soul needed this reckless abandon, even just for a day.

I bought a stroopwafel from a street vendor pushing a wooden cart toward the corner of the flower market. Village scenes were painted on the cart. One featured people skating on the canals, holding their hands behind their backs. The smell of the waffles had sold me—it was the smell of a bakery after cinnamon buns had just emerged from the oven. After one of the thin waffles was smeared with soft caramel, another was placed on top. They were made on the spot on a round griddle and served warm. I moaned with pleasure as I devoured this delight.

Afterward I meandered a bit, limiting myself to the small area that I was familiar with. Even still, it was better than being imprisoned in that hotel in Rotterdam. Feeling free and light, I was contemplating how easy it had been to come to Amsterdam on my own when I heard a mother raise her voice to her son in Dutch.

I glanced over to see a boy around eight. He wanted a stroopwafel and she wasn't going to buy him one. Suddenly he ran to the cart and began pounding on the side. As the mother grabbed him to pull him away, he kicked at her and yelled something that must have been mean because everyone around her froze for a second. The poor woman then dashed off in pursuit of her unruly boy.

I blinked back tears. Witnessing the scene had taken me right back to the first time I'd realized Dennis was "winning."

Troy was eight and it was his bedtime. Dennis happened to be in the living room at the time, which was rare. Normally he was up in his office, working on his computer. I was happy, thinking we might have some evening family time. After showering, Troy came into the living room. Dennis stopped channel surfing and settled on a scary movie, so I suggested to Troy that we go upstairs and read.

"I don't want to go upstairs," Troy protested. "Can I stay with you, Dad?"

"Of course, Troy. Your bedtime is when I say it is."

I looked at my husband with disbelief. He was well aware that our son went to bed at the same time every night.

"Troy," I said, more firmly. "It's almost time for bed. This is a scary movie that will give you bad dreams. Let's go upstairs." I picked up his slippers, which were beside the couch.

"I don't want to!" Troy yelled, while looking at his father. "You can't make me!"

Dennis had the biggest grin on his face.

"Dennis, you know this isn't a good idea," I pleaded.

"It's a good idea if I say it is, and if my son wants to watch this movie, then he'll watch this movie." He looked at Troy and winked.

That night, Troy woke up screaming. I ran into his room, and he told me he'd had a nightmare about aliens torturing him with needles. The dream mimicked a scene in the movie that he'd watched with his dad. While Dennis was sound asleep, I calmed Troy down with a warm cloth, hummed a James Taylor song softly and sat on his floor until he drifted off again.

It was the beginning of the unraveling. Of the slow dismantling of manners and work ethic, of perspective and appreciation.

From that point on, whenever Dennis was around, Troy would defy me while his father egged him on with a smirk of approval. No matter what I said to Dennis, he threw it in my face: "You're too domineering," or "You'll ruin the boy."

Eventually, I stopped saying anything. I stood by and watched as Dennis indulged our son and encased him in a world of affluence where no rules applied. By the time he turned sixteen, he was barely recognizable as the boy I'd known for the first eight years of his life.

Regardless, he was my son and I loved him.

As I stood there in the street in Amsterdam, regret rose in me like bile. I should have stood my ground when it came to Troy. *But how do you stand your ground with someone like Dennis?* another part of me countered. His manipulation skills were Jedi level.

I cursed the Dutch boy for triggering the festering memory. I'd tried to cover up the wound, but it was far from healed. As quickly as that, the feeling of lightness had drained out of me. I decided to call it a day and head back to Rotterdam.

Rather than walk back to the hotel, I headed in the direction of the Oude Kerk, which would cut down my walking distance by half. I knew how to find my way, and I no longer had any interest in enjoying Amsterdam or following Miriam on a whim. All I wanted was to return to my glass prison and wait out this trip. It had been a mistake to think that coming here would fix anything.

I thought of "The Rime of the Ancient Mariner," a poem by Samuel Taylor Coleridge that I'd read in junior college. It told the story of a captain who killed an albatross and was then forced by his crew to carry the massive bird around his neck as punishment. He carried the burden until he learned to have hope and pray again. While the poem was far too deep for me to understand on any literary level,

I was reminded of it now because I felt as though a larger-than-life weight had been thrown onto my shoulders—and I had no idea how to unburden myself. I didn't know how to find the strength to pray.

I suppose this is me just giving up again, but what's my alternative? Pretend that all the damage is just going to dissipate while I'm over here?

I'd had my fun, but it was time to return to Rotterdam and face my reality. I just wished I could talk to Troy, hear his voice. Look in his eyes. Of course, this was impossible. Dennis kept reminding me that I needed to accept the truth: Troy was no longer mine to love.

The weight on my shoulders increased.

I walked in the direction of the train station with my head down. I turned left at the Oude Kerk and quickly headed down the pedestrian street. Not far from the church, I glanced up to see the windows on the left. My shortcut had taken me straight through the Red Light District. Again! How was it that I kept ending up here? This time, I knew how to handle myself. It was just a few blocks.

Keeping my head down, I picked up my pace and tried to walk with intention, like a woman on her lunch break. A woman who was late for an appointment. A woman on her way home to her family. The street was used by people with no intention of looking for a sexual transaction. I was so focused on getting to the other end of the street that I didn't see her when she stepped into my path.

I ran into her, causing water to spill from the vase she was carrying.

"Miriam," I said with a gasp, before I could stop myself.

"Ken ik jou?" she asked with surprise, as she searched my face. When I didn't answer, she said, "Do I know you?"

"Sorry," I blurted in a panic, shaking my head before rushing off as fast as my feet would take me. As I turned the corner, I looked back to see Miriam, all magenta and black, pouring the remainder of the water in the vase into the canal.

13

Back Again

The entire train ride back to Amsterdam, I replayed the scene in my mind. Over and over. How embarrassing. Of all people to bump into. It was unfathomable. And then my awkward response. She must have been so confused to hear a perfect stranger say her name.

When I returned to the hotel, Dennis didn't ask me a single question about my day. He was all worked up about the merger, which was taking longer than expected. I couldn't even pretend to care. I felt as if I were moving along the edge of my life, not quite a part of it. Everything was far away.

Dennis had ordered room service, and he ate his hamburger on the bed while watching a documentary about the Russian railway system. He rested his plate on his belly, and every now and then, he brushed away crumbs that had accumulated on his chest.

In that moment, I was utterly unattracted to him in every way possible.

I sat beside him and picked at the burger he'd ordered me.

"We'll have to change our return flight," he said, his mouth half full of French fries that he'd doused in ketchup. "I need to stay longer."

"How much longer?"

"Maybe another week. I'll know more tomorrow." He paused and looked at me. "May have to spend Christmas here." He looked at me expectantly, seemingly waiting for my response.

I couldn't stop myself.

"But what about Troy?"

The muscles in his jaw tightened. "When are you going to come to terms with this, Beth," he said coldly. "Troy is no longer your concern. He's in a better place."

The words hit me like a blast of cold water. "You talk about him like he's dead!"

"He should be to you." He studied me for a moment, as if to see how his harsh words were landing, and then turned away and continued. "There's nothing I can do about it. If I could do something to make this different, I would. But I have no power here." He turned up the volume on the TV.

His words gave me pause. Did it bother him that he had no control? He was so used to being in control of everything, after all. Was his indifference a defense mechanism to ward off the feeling of helplessness? *Welcome to my world.* Helpless had become my middle name.

Perhaps I'd misjudged him, and he was living in his own hell. Perhaps he was being strong for me.

Why couldn't he let me into his world, let me support him when he was down? Maybe I needed to take the initiative. I went to give him a hug, but he just pushed the food tray toward me.

"Can you put that outside the door? I'm finished."

The next day, I got up after Dennis had left and sat on the bed staring at the train station. I wished it were a real spaceship that would fly away and take me with it.

Should I go to Amsterdam again today? The thought popped into my head unbidden.

I thought about the concierge at the hotel in Amsterdam and how he'd gone on about the extensive art in the Rijksmuseum.

You haven't seen that yet, I thought, bargaining with myself, looking for any excuse to get me back on that train. I could take in the Rijksmuseum and study the Dutch painters. Now that would be a fine distraction. I'd have the entire day to stand in line, if necessary, and I could certainly spend the whole day within the museum. The concierge had told me that it would take several days to scratch the surface of the place.

"You can learn a lot about the Dutch people through our art," he'd said. "We are pragmatic, frugal, honest, and realistic."

He'd explained that the Dutch artists featured in the museum tended to paint with a more lifelike style, concerned with the real world. Maybe seeing what the real world looked like in the Netherlands would help me face my real world. The one waiting back in the States.

Amsterdam it was! And this time, I'd do it with a little flair. Miriam appeared in my mind as I combed my wardrobe. I chose some heels, narrow plaid pants, a mint green cashmere sweater, and a matching scarf. While I didn't have a stylish hat or jacket to complete the outfit, I could perhaps buy one en route to the museum. So many shops offered a selection of chic clothing. I'd steer clear of the casual uniform of the women in my area of California. No exercise pants or active-wear tees, flip-flops or cross-trainers, hiking jackets or jeans. Looking at myself, I couldn't help but smile. I looked as if I fit in here.

Back on the train, I felt a sense of comfort, as if I'd been commuting to this city my whole life. I had my sudoku book but spent most of the time looking out the window instead. My heart jumped when I spotted a row of historic Dutch windmills in the distance. I'd thought they were only props in movies, but there they were, spinning slowly as the train zipped by. *How did I not notice these before?*

In the city, I easily found the red-bricked Rijksmuseum, as it was directly in front of the ice rink and the Van Gogh Museum. Luck was on my side, as the line wasn't long. Perhaps because it was a Monday morning. Within twenty minutes I was in. I decided on a headset because I wanted to take my time, learn something new, and keep my mind busy. The museum was overwhelmingly enormous. And the more I looked, the more I wanted to know.

I was drawn to a room full of paintings of tulips—paintings from the 1600s by Jacob Marrel and Hans Bollongier. I learned from my audio that tulips had been a valuable commodity in the seventeenth century.

Most of the tulips in these paintings were in vases, and the bends in the stems as well as the veins in the petals were remarkably detailed. There were paintings of singular tulips with insects resting on their petals and paintings of several tulips suspended in midair. The variety was impressive. My favorite tulip was the yellow one with red stripes and fringed petal edges. Maybe I'd buy some bulbs for the garden when I got home. And maybe I'd plant them myself. To hell with what Dennis said.

There were many paintings of white tulips with red stripes. Some of the tulips were lying on a surface as if being readied to be examined by a botanist, while others were arranged ornately. All of them looked as if they'd just been picked. They beckoned me closer. One of the conservators in the room watched me like a hawk as I stepped nearer to a canvas. I had to remind myself that I was looking at two-dimensional renderings.

What would he do if I got even closer and tried to smell the canvas? I thought with a chuckle. I could already see the headline: "American Woman Arrested for Art Vandalism."

I wandered around the room twice, feeling as if I were shopping at the flower market. Then I came upon a painting that made me pause. It featured not a tulip but a bunch of asparagus. This one had been painted in 1697 by Adriaen Coorte. I was mesmerized by how three-dimensional this two-dimensional painting looked. And the subject matter was so unusual. A plate of asparagus?

The audio explained that the subject matter was a symbol of wealth because it was an expensive food at the time. Some wealthy men commissioned painters to paint the vegetable and paid grandly for the finished product. *I wonder what Dennis would commission a painter to paint. Perhaps a portrait of himself?* I imagined the painter in his kitchen, watching his wife set out the meal, his hunger inspiring his realistic rendition of the platter. I wanted to reach out and grab a stalk—that's how real it looked.

Similarly inspired by the painting, my stomach began to growl. I glanced at my watch and my jaw dropped. I'd spent almost two hours in two adjoining rooms of the museum. I could have spent the rest of the day marveling at the optical illusions, but I needed to eat.

Maybe I'll find a restaurant and have a peaceful lunch today, I thought. Right now, that sounded preferable to the Christmas market. This side of town seemed quieter, and it was early enough that I'd miss the bustle of lunch hour.

After leaving the museum, I soon came upon a two-story home that had been renovated into a restaurant. The narrow old house had a unique facade with peaked rooflines. A server led me up a narrow set of wooden stairs that squeaked all the way. I was certain that he had to pick and choose which customers to seat on the second floor because the stairway was so cramped. He sat me at a table by a window that overlooked the canal, and I watched a couple get their picture taken on one of the many bridges that crossed it.

How charming.

I ordered lunch pancakes, which contained ham and asparagus and were drizzled with cream sauce. A specialty of the restaurant, according to the server. I chuckled at the coincidence. I couldn't remember the last time I'd eaten a dish containing asparagus.

The pancakes were delicious, and after I'd finished eating, I sat there feeling full—and not just from the food. I felt full of life. I'd taken a train to a city and visited a museum before eating lunch at a local restaurant. For some, this would be a typical occurrence, but for me, this was a big day. Today, I'd become part of the Amsterdam landscape. And today, I chose to congratulate myself for that rather than chastise myself for not having broadened my horizons sooner.

On my way back to the station, I went in the direction of the Westerkerk, which was labeled on my well-used map. On its steeple was a bright-blue crown gilded with gold. I'd seen it from the flower market on both occasions I'd visited it. I was getting better at navigating by church steeples and building facades within my limited perimeter. As I got closer, I noticed hundreds of people moving in a serpentine line on the other side of the canal. I stopped and peered in that direction. The area was roped off, and the line wound around the church. I hadn't realized it was such an attraction! The wait would be at least an hour. Then I noticed that the line was to get into the Anne Frank House, next door. I thought about the old man on the train and his reference to Anne Frank's house. He was right about one thing: A lot of people were willing to wait a long time to get in there. Perhaps on my next visit.

I continued walking and arrived at the station earlier than planned. What to do? The train had just left, and I had almost an hour to kill.

Without thinking about it, I found myself walking back in the direction of the Red Light District, still stubbornly refusing to acknowledge what was gnawing at my subconscious.

At the entrance to the district, you could be anywhere; it was charming and picturesque until you got to the windows. But even those seemed less daunting in the daylight. It seemed that many people used the street to get to where they were going: men, women, and children. I couldn't deny it was fascinating.

I decided to check in at that little store to see if any porcelain reindeer had arrived. At least that's what I told myself I was doing. I forced myself not to look in the direction of Miriam's window. Her curtain was drawn anyway.

I turned at the cheese store and was soon in front of Les Petites Chattes. To my disappointment, there were no ceramic reindeer in the window. As a matter of fact, none of the characters were left in the window: no ducks, no cats, no foxes, not even the live kitty. I did notice that the shop owner had created a lovely basket, complete with pinecones, shoes, the raggedy bear, and thick gold and blue velvet ribbons with tiny lights woven through them. A true decorating success. I contemplated telling her so, but she was busy fitting someone with a pair of boots, with her back to me.

Funny that I was feeling comfortable enough to assume that she'd care about my opinion on anything, let alone remember me!

My path back to the station crossed in front of Miriam's window, which was kitty-corner and across the canal from the cheese shop. From afar, I tried to focus my gaze on it. I could see someone in the window but couldn't tell if it was her. The closer I got, the harder it was to look inconspicuous. I certainly didn't want to be one of those "lookie-loos." Nor did I want to end my day with someone yelling at me or chasing me away with a broom.

I pretended to look for something in my bag, and when I looked up, there was a man standing in front of her door, his back to me. The rational part of my brain told me I had to move, but I was once again frozen in place, so I quickly rooted around in my bag again. The next time I looked up, the door opened and the man stepped in. Clear as day, I saw Miriam grab the red curtain and pull it across the window and door. Before she'd disappeared behind the curtain, I'd caught a glimpse of a soft smile on her face.

Exhaling, I got moving, crossing the bridge. I then turned left instead of right, heading away from the station. Again, I used the tower as a beacon to guide me to the Oude Kerk. I slowed to take another look at the bronze statue of the woman in the doorway standing proudly with her hands on her hips. This time, I read the small plaque at the bottom.

Respect sex workers all over the world.

I stared in surprise. The bronze statue that I'd thought

represented some heroic event in history was in honor of prostitutes!

Suddenly I thought of Tom, from the cheese shop, and how he'd been so protective of the women in the windows. He seemed to want to shield them from any ugliness on the outside of the glass. From the men in huddles, pooling money. From the people taunting and judging, even laughing as they walked by. Maybe even from the shock and awe on the faces of people like me, who'd never seen anything like this and didn't know what to think. I was certain no statue like this existed in America! It was so ironic to me that people like Tom would advocate for something that would be treated with contempt back home.

Near the Oude Kerke, I ducked into a café that advertised stroopwafels. When the server delivered my order, she instructed me to put the waffle on top of my coffee cup to soften the caramel. *How delightful!* I thought. *Such a practical use of the warmth.*

I followed her instructions, even dipped the waffle in my coffee to soften it further, but I had to admit that I preferred the ones at the Christmas market, freshly made and oozing with gooeyness.

A cozy storefront with *PIC&PROUD* in the window caught my eye as I left the café. In the window was also a small replica of *Belle*, the statue I'd seen in front of the church. Flower boxes filled with round, shiny blue and gold holiday ornaments decorated the windowsill. Walking over to take a closer look, I read the chalkboard beside a small table and realized that this wasn't another café, as I'd thought, but a place where you could book tours of the Red Light District. *PIC* stood for "Prostitution Information Center," and *Proud* spoke for itself. Hanging in the window were T-shirts featuring *Belle* and carry bags that said *STIGMA KILLS*. I couldn't help smirking at the thought of how Dennis would react if I returned to the hotel with a *Belle* shirt and wore it to bed. Would he even know what it represented?

The next tour was at 5:00 p.m. Who took these tours? I wondered. Were they about education or "window-shopping"? The notion of people touring the Red Light District was absurd to me. I imagined a man pointing out various women in the windows with a wooden cane. He'd stop and let the crowd gather before announcing, "Now, here's a real opportunity for those of you who like a red head." The crowd would nod, and then they'd move on to the next window.

Ridiculous! What did Miriam think of the tours? What did Tom think? This place had truly turned upside down the world I'd thought I'd known.

My head was already in a spin when I saw a woman come out from a nearby building pushing a set of connected strollers that looked like a small train filled with eight small children. They headed in the direction of the windows. Looking in the opposite direction, I saw a place called the Museum of Prostitution. All the contrasts here felt preposterous.

Time to go back to the train station. I'd pushed the boundaries of my comfort zone as far as I could.

It didn't take long to catch up with the train of strollers as I walked, and I had to wonder if the little ones had any notion of what those women in the windows were doing with hardly any clothes on in the dead of winter. Just then, I saw a little hand rise from the stroller and wave. One of the window ladies returned the favor and blew a kiss to the stroller train. I frowned. *How odd.* As I got closer to the strollers, I could hear the woman pushing them humming a lovely tune, as if she were strolling on a path lined with tulips through a well-groomed park. It struck me as ridiculous that anyone would stroll little ones through a street of prostitution but here it was being done right before my eyes and no one seemed to react to it but me!

Musing on how peculiar this all was, I didn't realize I was in front of Miriam's window until the door opened and out came a man in a suit—the same man I'd seen enter thirty minutes earlier. He had salt-and-pepper hair and deep blue eyes. He waved goodbye to her as if saying farewell to a dear friend, and Miriam blew him a kiss, which he caught in midair and returned to her with a big smile on his face.

"*Wat wil je van me?*"

There was Miriam, staring right at me. Once again, I'd been so preoccupied with their intimate exchange that I'd forgotten to keep moving.

"Sorry?" was all I could think to say. What had my silly, obsessive curiosity gotten me into? Had I crossed the line? Would Tom be coming over with a wheel of cheese to knock some sense and respect into me?

"What do you want from me?" she said, with a matter-of-fact look on her face, her tone suggesting she was waiting for me to tell her about the last item on a shopping list.

"Nothing," I blurted. "I'm sorry." I started to walk away but she caught my arm, not roughly but with purpose.

"I do not have time now, but if you come back tomorrow, I will meet you at the cafe at the corner"—she pointed down the street—"and I will tell you whatever you want to know."

"I don't understand . . . ?"

"Meet me there at eleven and don't be late. I have work to do." She looked at me pointedly. "You know what I mean?"

"I really—"

"Listen, I do not have time now. My three o'clock is always early." She shot me a quick smile and walked back to her window.

I felt an urge to follow her and tell her that there had been some sort of misunderstanding. That there was nothing she needed to tell me about. But before I could make a move, a dapper older gentleman in a plaid woolen blazer and a flat gray cap sauntered in the direction of Miriam's door.

From her window, Miriam waved me away, as if she were shooing away a pest.

Tomorrow, I was going to meet Miriam at eleven o'clock at a café down the street and she was going to tell me whatever I wanted to know. I had no idea what that was, but I found myself looking forward to finding out.

14

INTRODUCTIONS

I floated through the next several hours, the prospect of meeting up with Miriam consuming me. A week ago, I'd never have considered it, but apparently I'd evolved into a new version of myself: Beth 2.0!

When Dennis returned to the hotel, he was in a foul mood, a result of the stall in the merger. Usually the recipient of his frustration, left deflecting caustic remarks, I felt invulnerable to his antics that evening. I didn't engage in his rant, didn't question his comments. Didn't respond much in general. I just shook my head and threw out an occasional "uh-huh." The funny thing was that Dennis didn't even notice. Once he'd unloaded his annoyance, he planted himself on the bed and ordered room service: another hamburger and French fries to devour. I ordered Erwtensoep, which was a thick pea soup that I had seen on the menu when I had lunch in Amsterdam. Dennis scowled at me and shook his head, obviously not pleased with my decision.

The next morning, I greeted the day like a best friend, eager to return to Amsterdam. I headed to the train station at nine o'clock, where I found myself among the last of the Tuesday-morning commuters. On the train, I had to stand until the first stop. Once I settled into a seat, I took notice of the weather for the first time. There was a swatch of dark clouds in the distance. I hoped I'd dressed appropriately.

I arrived at the cafe early and paused outside the door, consumed in my thoughts. I'd had to pass Miriam's window to get there, and the curtain had been pulled shut.

Wow, nothing like starting the morning on your back.

Was there a proper time to engage in sex? Nighttime came to mind. Who would want to have sex at ten o'clock in the morning? Did she get up and shower and then go have sex? Then what did she do? Go home and shower? Where did she live? Was the window her home?

My heart rate picked up and my palms started to sweat despite the cold air. What was I doing? I didn't belong here. This was a big mistake. I was still standing outside the cafe, contemplating a quick exit, when I heard her distinctive voice.

"Hoi."

I turned to see her walking toward me in a gray fitted sweater dress and a black cape draped over her shoulder. It looked as if she'd taken quite a bit of time positioning the cape perfectly so that it stayed in place. A stylish accent to her already stylish look. She looked nothing like a woman who worked behind the glass.

"Hello."

"Shall we go in?" She reached for the door, and we entered the busy café and headed for a table in the back. She ordered coffee and cheese toast. I followed her lead and ordered the same.

"OK," she said, once our server had left. "What can I do for you?" She looked at me as though we were discussing a business venture.

"I'm not sure what you mean by that," I said hesitantly.

"I believe you Americans say 'This is not my first rodeo.'" She gave me a small smile.

"I'm sorry," I said, deciding then and there that honesty would be the best way to defuse the situation. "There's been a big misunderstanding. My name is Beth, and I'm here with my husband on a business trip."

"OK, I don't have all day to sit around and talk nice with you," she said, annoyance creeping into her tone. "Let's get to the point. You tell me who you want to know about, and we'll get on with our business."

My eyebrows rose. "No one! I don't want to know about anyone."

Our order was delivered, and I quickly took a sip of the coffee for courage.

"I see. So you have been lurking around my window for days now and following me at the flower market, and I am supposed to think this is a coincidence?"

She took a bite of her cheese toast, and the crunch made me wince. It resembled the chomp in her voice.

"I wasn't following you, I promise," I said, my cheeks

getting hotter by the minute.

"Why don't we just get right to it. Who are you working for and who do you want to know about?" She looked me straight in the eyes and didn't blink. When I didn't answer, she continued. "By the way, whatever firm you work for should be informed that you are terrible at being discreet."

"Firm? Sorry, you've lost me again."

"Wives hire private detectives like you to get dirt on their husbands. I know the drill. I have no problem giving you information as long as you stop stalking me."

What? I stifled a nervous giggle. "Oh, no, seriously. My name is Beth. My husband and I are here . . . well, we were here in Amsterdam for three days, and now we're in Rotterdam as he settles a merger." Miriam didn't look satisfied, so I went on. "I've been spending my days in Amsterdam, and I happened to run into you on more than one occasion. You seem to get around—" I caught myself and blushed. "Oh, I didn't mean it that way."

With that, she threw her head back and laughed so hard that people in the room glanced at us. Unsure whether her laughter was from rage or humor, I waited, anxiously nibbling on my cheese toast.

"So, you do not work for a PI firm?"

"No."

"And there is no one you are looking into?"

"No."

She laughed again.

This time I smiled and shrugged.

"Well, then. Apologies for accusing you wrongfully."

She smiled back and offered her hand, immediately lightening the mood.

I reached out and shook it. "Apology accepted."

"You see," she said, taking a sip of her coffee, "I have had a few incidents with PIs, so I decided that as soon as I suspected I was being followed, I would jump on it and get the business done. Since you are not one of them, I have to ask—why do you spend so much time in the Red Light District?"

I swallowed my mouthful and gathered myself. "Well, that's a great question. It's my first time in Amsterdam. My first time really anywhere, actually. And I figured out how to navigate this town using landmarks. The big church—"

"Oude Kerk."

"Yes, it's one of my landmarks. I actually ran into you for the first time by the brass statue in the ground."

A look of recognition crossed her face. "Oh yes, I remember."

I thought about our first meeting, a little over a week ago. How was I sitting here having coffee and toast with a prostitute whom I'd initially thought was some important lady?

Miriam took the last bite of her cheese toast then brushed a crumb off her sweater. "That is a story I have never heard. I guess I may have a case of paranoia, then."

I held my tongue. It would be creepy to tell her that I'd felt drawn to her. That I was curious about the way she moved in and out of her worlds: the world of the Red Light District and the world the rest of us lived in.

"How many times have you been approached by detectives?" I asked, and then quickly added, "If you don't mind my asking."

"Four times. It is a tricky business I work in." She gave me a gentle, disarming smile that melted away my remaining anxiety. I supposed a smile like this would be necessary in her "business."

"Has it ever turned out bad for you?" I asked, feeling more emboldened. She was so easy to talk to.

She pursed her lips, wearing a thoughtful expression. "Most of the time it works out badly for my customer, not for me. But there was one customer's wife who decided to show up and spray-paint my window."

"Oh wow, that's terrible! What did she write?"

"I would rather not say. Not language fit for a lady. Plus, it does not translate well into English. It had something to do with a donkey and a wooden spoon."

This time it was my turn to laugh, and she quickly joined me.

I didn't want our time to end. It had been so long since I'd had someone to talk to, someone to share coffee with. I didn't have friends. I had acquaintances, through Dennis, and these people, most of whom were at least ten years my senior, were so wrapped up in climbing the corporate ladder or acting like spouses of upper management that a natural exchange was impossible. I loathed these interactions.

"How long have you been doing . . ." I stumbled, not knowing how to phrase it. "Working here?"

Miriam tensed up again and looked me square in the

eyes. "Are you sure you are not a detective? Perhaps you should show me the contents of your purse. You wouldn't happen to have a recording device in there?"

"Oh, gosh no!" I immediately opened my bag and offered it to her. "Here, look for yourself."

She leaned over and rifled through it before settling back in her chair. "OK, I guess you are clean."

"You're so easy to talk to," I said apologetically. "I got ahead of myself. I'm sorry."

"I will let it slide. This time." She smiled that disarming smile and studied my face. "So where in America are you from, Beth?"

"California."

"And what do you think of our fine city?" She took the last sip of her coffee and gently pushed away the cup and saucer.

"Oh, I've loved it," I gushed.

"I know you've been to the flower market," she said, with a wink. "Where else have you ventured?"

"Hmm, the Van Gogh Museum, the Rijksmuseum, the ice rink. I've also been to the Christmas market, the city center . . ." I trailed off, wondering if mentioning where I'd eaten would make me sound small-town.

"And a canal ride? I am sure you did that."

"Actually I didn't. The weather hasn't been great."

"The canal boats have covers. You Americans are such delicate flowers," she said, but her tone was playful again. "Perhaps next time you come to Amsterdam, we can take a canal ride together. You have to experience it."

"I would love to," I blurted. "When?" I flushed, suddenly afraid that my eagerness would scare her and that her offer had been only a polite gesture and not a real proposal. But to my pleasant surprise, she responded by taking out her phone.

"Let me see. What about the day after tomorrow? Will you be here?"

"Yes, I will!" I said, suddenly so grateful that Dennis was extending the trip at least a week.

"Shall we say eleven o'clock? This way, we avoid the morning crowd. I will clear my afternoon calendar."

I stifled another giggle. She sounded like someone in upper management at Dennis's firm, yet she was so far from that line of work. Or was she? I wanted to learn more about Miriam. She seemed so comfortable in her own skin.

"Eleven o'clock sounds great. Where shall I meet you?" I asked, not wanting to assume that I should knock on her glass door.

"Let's meet at the dock in front of the train station. It will be my treat. My way of giving you a true Amsterdam experience. I would like to make up for my assumption that you were a pesky private investigator."

I beamed. "I look forward to it."

She looked down at her phone to check the time and then seemed to be doing some mental math. When our server came with our bill, I took it. "I'd like to pay. This has been so nice for me. I don't get a chance to get out with women much."

She smiled. "Well, Beth from California, thank you for

the coffee and cheese toast. And thank you for not being a detective. If you had been, I'd definitely encourage you to find another line of work."

I chuckled. I could only imagine how much I stood out as I wandered the Red Light District.

"I rarely see women in that job, in fact. Men are much more subtle." She shook her finger at me. "That is not a sexist comment but a fact of life as I see it. In my business, it is important to be clear and direct about everything." She paused before continuing. "I look forward to our ride on the canals the day after tomorrow. Can I walk you to the train? I am heading that way."

When we stepped outside, the sky was darker and the wind had picked up. Snow seemed imminent. I buttoned up my coat and tightened my scarf. It was the coldest weather I'd experienced since arriving in the country. As Miriam and I walked, she talked about some of the buildings and explained that the floating canopy bed in the canal was part of an art exhibit.

When we passed the whiskey store, she waved at the old man behind the counter. He waved back as though acknowledging a highly regarded citizen. I glanced at her. She'd pulled her hair over one shoulder and looked like a model—poised, classy, confident, beautiful. How could it be that she'd return to that window and offer herself up to any man who offered money? It didn't make sense in my mind. Everything I knew about prostitutes had led me to believe they were dirty, sleazy, and indecent. Yet here she was, walking me to the train station as if she were a representative of the city of Amsterdam, revered by all who crossed her path. *She even has a cape like the guides used to wear in Disneyland*, I thought with a chuckle.

As we neared the train station, snow began falling in a light sprinkle. Snowflakes collected on Miriam's cape, and she looked up and smiled at the tiny white flecks. She was so genuinely joyful. How could that be?

"*Doei*," Miriam said, with a wave.

"Sorry? I don't understand."

"*Doei* means 'goodbye.' You really need to work on your Dutch," she said, patting me on the back.

"OK, dooo eeee," I said, and she gave me a thumbs-up before turning to leave.

I was grateful to be on the train ahead of rush hour. The quiet gave me space to digest my time with Miriam. How lucky for me that she'd thought I was a private detective! I probably never would have officially met her otherwise. I still had so many questions I wanted to ask her. My fascination with her and her lifestyle aside, it had been so nice to have a genuine conversation with another woman—a taste of what it might be like to have a friend. Someone with whom I could share the events of the day. The last real friendship I'd had had been with Sheila, back when I worked for the company, and that hadn't lasted long because Dennis found her too common.

What would he think about Miriam?

I already knew. I planned to keep our meetups to myself.

The snow had turned to rain by the time the train approached Rotterdam. Feeling energized by my day, I decided to work out and then use the sauna.

In the hotel lobby, I shook out my hair. The rain had done a number on it. As I passed the front desk, a young man in a double-breasted red jacket with gold buttons slipped out from behind it to meet me.

"Hello, Mrs. Strum. Here is the phone number your husband requested."

"Oh," I said, my brow furrowing. "OK." I took the slip of paper containing a phone number that looked American. I began to walk away but felt pulled to ask. "Any idea what this number is?"

"Oh yes. It is your son's new number. He has been moved."

15

No Contact

I got in the elevator and gripped the railing, feeling as though I might pass out. The slip of paper in my hand had become moist from my sweaty palm. My son. This number was my son's number. He'd been moved.

What did that mean?

Dennis had told me it was impossible to contact him. He'd told me that I could no longer be a part of his life. And here I was, holding his number. I wanted to run upstairs and call it immediately, but I had to consider the fact that Dennis had withheld this information from me.

What did that mean?

One thing was certain: the reception guy had screwed up big time.

When I got into the room, I went straight to the phone. I lay the strip of paper beside it on the table and stared at it.

Should I call? Would Troy answer? Was that possible? If so, why had this been kept from me?

I picked up the phone, pressed nine for an outside line, and then dialed the number, my fingers trembling. While the call connected, I felt as if I were trying to contain an explosion in my body. Every muscle was tense. I waited to hear his voice. The voice that I'd built my life around. The voice that brought me great joy. And great sorrow.

After what felt like a lifetime, there was a click followed by a busy signal. I hung up and sat down on the bed. It was two o'clock in the afternoon, which meant it was five o'clock in the morning in California, if that was where he was. I knew five o'clock was early, but I was not longer thinking in rational terms. I just needed to hear his voice.

You need to calm down, I told myself. If Troy had picked up, I would have sounded stressed out, and stress was the last thing I wanted to convey. Was Troy even capable of picking up? I felt helpless, stupid for not knowing.

Taking a deep breath, I tried again and got a busy signal. What did that mean? Was I dialing correctly? Moments later, I dialed a third time, pausing between each number to ensure accuracy. A pause and a busy signal were all I got.

I lay back on the bed and exhaled.

It had been almost a month since the accident. Almost a month since I'd seen my son. I thought of the night that Dennis got the call.

Our home phone rang, and Dennis picked it up. He

held the receiver to his ear and listened for several seconds.

"Wait a minute, let me write that down" he said, while walking from the kitchen to the den. I heard him rip a piece of paper from a pad and thank the person on the other end of the line.

Then he came into the living room, where I'd been reading. "I have to get to the office," he said. "Something came up that needs my attention."

He didn't come home that night. In the morning, he called to say that he'd fallen asleep on the couch in his office and would be home at the usual time.

"Is everything all right?" I asked.

"I'll fill you in when I get home," he replied curtly.

I could only assume he'd been dealing with some incompetent employee who'd screwed something up. He was the fix-it man at WTS.

In the meantime, I had a problem of my own to deal with—Troy hadn't come home. I hadn't heard from him since he left to meet a friend the previous evening. It was unlike him.

I went into my son's room and wondered if a tornado had passed through. Clothes were strewn all over the floor and the bed. His chair was a heap of shirts and jackets, and his dresser drawers were all half open. This wasn't a surprise to me. Troy's room looked like this most of the time. Teenagers!

I searched for the calendar that I'd given him to keep track of his class schedule. On the wall by his bed, where I'd put it, there was only an empty nail. Peeking under the bed, I spotted the calendar and pulled it out. It hadn't been marked so offered no clues as to his whereabouts. Under the bed was also an empty plastic baggie with what looked like remnants of dried herbs. Against the far wall lay a few empty bottles as well as several small orange pill containers. He hadn't needed a prescription in over a year, since his bout with strep throat. A jolt of alarm went through me. I'd need to examine those containers more carefully, but first, I needed to make sure he was safe.

I remembered the last argument I'd had with Troy. It had been about keeping his room clean. After several back and forths—respect for the house versus personal freedom—Troy hit the usual nerve: "I don't care what you say. Dad is fine with it." That was always the closer. I'd known then that I'd been beaten. There was nothing I could do about it because Dennis wouldn't support me. Quite the opposite. He'd ridicule me, and he and Troy would leave the room laughing.

I could only hope that we'd be able to work together on the issue of what I'd found in Troy's room.

I called Troy's cell phone several times, but it always went right to voicemail. Finally, feeling desperate, I left a message: "Troy, this is your mom. Please call home. I'm worried about you."

I immediately wished I hadn't said that. It sounded so pathetic and would likely drive him farther away. I hated feeling this helpless. How had I become so ill-equipped as a mother?

When Dennis came home, he seemed tired. I asked

him about work, and he was quick to respond, assuring me everything was all right.

I couldn't contain myself any longer. "Dennis, I'm worried about Troy. He didn't come home last night. Did he tell you where he was going?"

"Oh, I know. You don't need to be worried about him," he said, not meeting my gaze. "Everything is under control."

"What do you mean? Have you heard from him? He hasn't answered my calls!" I stared at him, anxious for an answer, but his face was void of any emotion.

When he spoke again, it was with an eerily calm voice. A voice that I didn't recognize.

"Troy was in an accident last night, but he's OK."

"WHAT! What are you talking about?"

"He was driving and got into an accident with an old lady. Everyone is OK."

He walked to the dry bar to pour himself a drink, and that's when I noticed he was wearing the clothes he'd been wearing when he left the house the previous evening. He had extra shirts at the office for when work emergencies came up. Had he even gone to the office?

"Where is he? I want to see him." I started moving toward the front door, but Dennis stopped me with a hand on my arm.

"That's not possible, Beth. But he's fine. Everyone is fine."

"Why is it not possible?" I asked, tears running down my face. "I need to see my son. Where is he?"

Dennis grabbed both my arms firmly, so I was facing

him. "Listen to me. I would take you there if it would do any good, but it won't. Troy is fine."

"But why can't I see him? Dennis, this isn't fair. I want to know where my son is."

"You want to know what isn't fair?" he said, anger flaring in his eyes.

I widened my own in response.

"What isn't fair is that he sustained a concussion and when he woke up and the nurse mentioned your name, he became hysterical and had to be sedated. That's what's not fair. What have you done to our son to make him go crazy like that?"

I blinked, at a loss for words, thoughts, feelings. My son had become hysterical at the mention of me. None of this made sense. Troy and I had had our problems lately, but I wasn't a threat to him. Never had been. I couldn't fathom him responding that way.

I shook my head. "I want to see him, Dennis. Where is he?"

"You can't. It's impossible. There's been a directive written to prevent you from visiting him until he's of sound mind and body. We have to respect the hospital's wishes."

Sobs overtook me, and he wrapped me in his arms. "There, there, Beth. Everything will be all right. Just trust me."

I melted in his embrace. I sobbed for my son and his wounds unknown to me. I sobbed for the old woman I didn't know. I sobbed for my broken heart and at the thought that I'd possibly caused this.

Then Dennis guided me into the living room and had me lie down on the couch. He sat beside me and stroked my head. "Everything will be all right. You'll see. Let me get you something to calm you down. I think I have something upstairs that will do the trick."

He started for the stairs.

"What about the old lady?" I asked.

"Stupid woman," he spat. "She shouldn't have been driving. Anyway, she's fine."

"Was it her fault?" I looked up at Dennis, who looked away and shook his head.

"What do you think?" he said. "Jesus."

The next day, I found a receipt for a tow-truck service in the pocket of Dennis's pants as I was preparing a load of laundry.

When Dennis came home that evening, I brandished the receipt, determined to find out more. "Where's the car?"

Dennis had bought Troy the cherry-red convertible for his sixteenth birthday. Troy had actually wanted a little truck, but his father had insisted that a convertible was a "chick magnet."

"Any son of mine will drive only the best," he'd said. The car had been in our son's possession for only a few short months.

"How much damage?" I bit my lip, waiting for the details.

"Totaled," Dennis said, in a tone that suggested he wouldn't be elaborating.

The next day, in desperation, I called the closest hospitals in town and asked for Troy Strum's room, only to be told that no one by that name had been admitted in the last week. I then called all the hospitals in a twenty-five-mile radius and got the same answer.

Where the hell was my son?

The days marched on. Every evening I'd ask Dennis about Troy and would get a one- or two-word answer. Whenever the home phone rang, I'd jump to get it, in hopes it was Troy. I began to have trouble sleeping, and when I finally slept, I'd have nightmares featuring Troy: Troy being attacked by zombies, Troy being dragged down the street by a horse, Troy being pushed off a cliff. I'd wake up leaking tears.

Even still, all I could squeeze out of Dennis was that Troy was getting better and that I had to be patient. He reminded me that I was being selfish, that I had to think of what was best for Troy. In the days leading up to Thanksgiving, I avoided my mother and was relieved when she called me to say she'd decided to visit my aunt in Utah. Dennis and I ate rotisserie chicken from a local eatery in front of the TV.

By the time December rolled around, I could barely function. I felt as if I were sleepwalking. I was going through the motions, always praying, *Let this be the day that Troy comes home.* And then the trip to Amsterdam had come up.

I'd been so naïve to think that I'd be able to mend the void in my heart, the missing family member, the love of my life.

I tried the number one more time with no luck. I needed to come up with a plan—quickly. This was my opportunity to reach Troy without Dennis's interference.

In a flash of inspiration, I wrote down the number on another piece of paper but transposed the last four numbers. I'd leave this wrong number for Dennis to find. Two could play this game.

I suddenly felt stronger.

After hiding the real number in the toe of one of my high heels, I changed my clothes and headed to the gym for a workout, as planned, and it ended up being an out-of-body experience. I ran and pedaled and lifted as if I did so daily, fully immersed in the experience, working off the tension, the stress, the sadness.

While employed at WTS, I'd often used the company's gym. A trainer there had given me a personalized workout circuit, which I did every other day, but then I got married and stopped working, which meant I no longer had access to that gym. I was left with adapting his workout on my living room floor when Troy was at school.

My body rained sweat as I processed my frustration on the bike. Mirrors surrounded me, and when I caught sight of my reflection, I almost didn't recognize myself. I wore a look of determination.

Things needed to change. And the only way that was going to happen was if I took charge. *I* needed to change.

When I got back to the room, Dennis was there and the slip of paper that I'd left on the desk for him was gone. He came out of the bathroom with his shirt unbuttoned. I hesitated.

"Hi."

"Where were you?" he asked.

"Working out." *Isn't that obvious?*

My life was filled with this kind of redundant chatter.

"Well, we're going to meet Max and his wife in the restaurant downstairs, so you better clean up." He picked up the remote and the TV clicked on.

"I'm not sure I'm up for that. I'm feeling beat."

The words were out before I realized I'd uttered them. I was treading on new ground. I'd never questioned his demands. If he wanted me to go somewhere, I went. If he wanted me to buy something, I bought it. If he wanted to withhold information about our son, he did exactly that and I accepted it.

Why?

"Don't be silly, Beth," he said, not looking at me. "You'll feel better after a shower. You better get a move on."

"I really don't feel up to it, Dennis." My voice didn't sound like my own.

"Never mind that, Beth. I'm not really asking you. Max is bringing his wife and I will be bringing mine. That's how it goes. What's gotten into you?" He glanced in my direction only briefly before returning his attention to the screen. I was losing ground. I didn't yet have the skills to maintain my position with him. Or did I?

"The front desk gave me a phone number to give to you," I said, feigning nonchalance. "I left it on the desk. Did you get it?"

"Yes, thanks."

"Whose number is it?" I asked, hoping for but not

expecting the truth.

He waved his hand dismissively, his eyes still on the TV. "It's the number of a local dry cleaner. I need to get my suit cleaned. This trip is going to be longer than I thought, as you know."

And there it was. The lie had left his lips so easily I wondered if the man at the reception desk had gotten it wrong. I wondered if it was, indeed, the number of a dry cleaner. I'd only gotten a busy signal so far, after all.

Doubt crept back into my head like a fog. Was I imagining things? Had the man at the reception desk actually said "your son"? Or had my mind been longing to hear those words so much that I'd imagined them? What reason did my husband have to lie to me, anyway?

I decided to take a shower to avoid further tension. But as I massaged shampoo into my hair, my mind continued to race. While Dennis was in the room, I couldn't determine whether he was lying or not. I'd have to wait until tomorrow. Until then, I'd put on my happy face and assume my position beside him.

As the evening progressed, I started hoping that when I called that number again, I'd find out it was a dry cleaner. I didn't want to have any more doubts. If Troy did end up answering, then every detail that Dennis had fed me over the last few weeks might be a lie.

And what would that mean?

As soon as we left the restaurant after dinner, Dennis expressed his displeasure with my lack of attentiveness. Frankly, I couldn't remember a word of the discussion. My need to know whether Dennis had lied to me had become all-consuming. I'd begun thinking about every single piece of information he'd given me: Troy had become hysterical at the mention of my name. There was a directive forbidding me to see him. Was any of it true? If not, I'd been robbed of a month with my son. The thought made my blood boil.

The next morning, I stayed in bed until Dennis left for work. By my calculations, it was eleven thirty at night in California—that was, if Troy was even in California. He could be in Africa for all I knew. Still, I'd wait to call.

Outside, the sky was dark gray and promised more cold weather. Needing to burn some time, I decided to go to the gym again. My muscles were sore, but the ache was a welcome distraction from the pain in my heart. The pain of uncertainty. The gym was empty except for the cleaning lady, who came in to dust the large plants in the corners.

Once back in the room, I noticed that I'd been gone only an hour and a half. What to do? There was a hot tub next to the gym, but it was usually full of mothers and children, so I decided against it.

Maybe a bath? The amenities in the room were ample, but instead of bubble bath, body wash and body oil had been supplied. This meant that I wouldn't have any bubbles to hide under. I almost opted for a shower instead, but a defiant voice in my head challenged me to go for it.

As I submerged myself in the hot water that smelled of lavender, I felt some of my tension loosen, so I sank lower, laid back, and let the heat soothe my achy muscles. I'd exercised more in the last few days than I normally would in a week.

My body told me in no uncertain terms that I was a bit out of shape, and I promised myself to step up my game—not because I wanted to look a certain way, necessarily, but because I was tired of feeling inadequate. I wanted to feel strong.

I glanced down at my naked body stretched out in the tub and forced myself to scan my figure from my chest to my stomach to my toes. It was startling to view myself this way. Once again, a disheartening thought settled itself in my mind: *If I were desirable, then I wouldn't be the only thirty-eight-year-old woman on the earth who hasn't had sex in years, so many years.*

Hoping to drown this thought out, I grabbed the body wash and mindfully scrubbed my arms, my chest. I made my way down. As I did so, a new appreciation for my body emerged. It did so much for me, and it felt good to take care of it. Then another thought occurred to me—maybe the way I felt about my body was simply another hold that Dennis had over me. Maybe I wasn't as repulsive as I thought. Maybe he reinforced my insecurity to maintain control.

When I stepped out of the bathtub, I dried myself slowly and then went to put on my robe but stopped. Several days ago, I hadn't been able to look at my reflection in the bathroom mirror. Now here I was, gathering strength. With my back to the mirror, I glanced over my shoulder and let the robe drop so that I could see my backside. Then I let it drop all the way to the floor.

An overwhelming wave of awkwardness swept over me—so powerful that I leaned down quickly and pulled the robe up and secured it.

Too much too soon, Beth.

Still, something had dislodged itself in my way of thinking, and I liked the result. I felt freer.

I retrieved the piece of paper with the phone number from my shoe. And then, taking a deep breath, I dialed the number again and waited. As much as I hoped Dennis wasn't lying, in this moment, all I wanted was to hear my son's voice. There was a click, a pause, more clicking, and then the line went dead. I hung up with a sigh.

I tried again. More clicking. Then, all of a sudden, a voice.

"Sunrise Ranch."

"Hello," I said quickly, my heart rate picking up, "I'm trying to reach Troy Strum." I placed my hand over my mouth. I felt as if I might throw up.

"Patients cannot take calls for another forty-five minutes," the woman said. "Who's calling?"

"Beth Strum. I'm Troy's mother."

There was a pause that I interpreted as time she was taking to locate him or his chart or his status. I wanted to ask her a million questions but forced myself to be patient. For a moment, the air on the line was so silent I wondered if we'd gotten disconnected. Then I heard a quick inhale, and the line went dead for real.

I quickly tried the number again. And again. I couldn't get through. That was it. Not even a click.

I crawled back into bed, unable to face another day not hearing my son's voice.

When I woke, the light in the room had changed. I'd

slept for hours. I got up and looked out the window at the train station. People were hustling down the steps from the station into the underground tunnel that crossed the street, and the sidewalk was crawling with bodies moving in every direction. *The workday must be coming to an end*, I thought.

Somehow, watching the swarm of bodies calmed me, helped me loosen the tightness in my neck. I was considering another attempt at calling Troy when I saw a man who looked just like Dennis walk out of the tunnel. He had the same gait, wore the same suit, held the same type of briefcase. He was walking toward the hotel. It *was* Dennis.

I sat on the bed. Why would Dennis be coming from the train? The company car always picked him up and dropped him off. He never failed to express his distaste for public transportation: "The working man's solution to getting around."

I waited and waited, for what seemed like far longer than it should have taken him to reach our room. What was I thinking? *I must have been seeing things. I really need to get a grip.* Actually, I really needed to get home, so I could wait for Troy. Maybe I could convince Dennis to put me on a plane tonight. Before I could think any further about it, the door clicked and Dennis walked in.

"Oh, it's you," I said, flustered. The implications of Dennis's walking through the door at that moment were daunting.

He scoffed. "Who did you think it would be? Fabio?"

"Are you early? I guess the time got away from me. How did you get to the hotel?"

"What do you mean?" He tossed his briefcase on the desk and took off his suit jacket. "I got here like I always do."

"So you didn't take the train?" I asked, desperate for the confirmation.

He turned and glared at me. "Why would I take the train? I hate the train. The train is filthy."

"Hmm." Maybe I really had taken flight from reality and was fabricating trouble where there was none. Dennis always said I did that. But something wasn't sitting right. I decided to take another route.

"Did you get a hold of the dry cleaner?"

"What?"

"You know, the number that you got from the front desk?" I lay back on the bed, propping myself up with my pillow, trying to act naturally.

"Oh, yes, the dry cleaner. I had the driver drop off my suit after he took me to the office. He's the nicest guy. His wife thinks one of their pet rabbits is pregnant," he said with a chuckle.

And there it was. My proof. I'd given him a fake number. He was lying.

"Which suit did you take in?" I managed to say, trying not to let my dismay show.

"The brown one."

"When will it be ready?"

"Day after tomorrow. The driver will pick it up for me." He frowned. "Why all the interest in my suit?"

My husband had lied to me in a way that suggested he was reading the ingredients from a recipe. Calmly. Methodically.

"I was thinking that we could go out tonight," he continued. "The concierge said there's a nice restaurant at the end of the street."

He'd lied to me so easily, as if he'd been doing it all his life. *He probably has*, I thought.

"Beth. I'm talking to you! Dinner? What the hell? Is it too much to ask for a response?"

"I don't feel like going out" was all I could muster in response. What I wanted to do was pick up the lamp and throw it at him.

"I'm going to wash up and then we can go check it out," he said, as if he hadn't heard me, then headed to the bathroom and closed the door.

He turned on the water. And in that moment, I hated myself almost as much as I hated him.

I managed to put on some clothes, and when he came out of the bathroom, he stared at me. I was sitting on the bed, staring into space.

"Go brush your hair. You look like a crazy person. And get your jacket, Beth. It's cold outside."

When I opened the closet to retrieve my jacket, I found it right next to the brown suit he'd said was at the dry cleaner.

16

Paper Trail

I never would have guessed it was possible to get so lost in my life, to feel so defenseless that I would have no idea how to proceed, but here I was. I had allowed my husband to control me. For years. I could see that now. And I had no idea how to rectify the situation. It was as if he had a command station where he programmed my actions for the day, and I then responded accordingly, like a droid.

He'd lied to me. There was no question about that. The bigger issue was what exactly he'd lied to me about. I had no idea how to find out. His lie about the phone number had opened a chasm of uncertainty. I didn't know what was real and what was fabricated, altered to meet the needs of Dennis and leave me in the dark.

I had no idea what, in my life, was true anymore.

I hardly slept that night and remained in bed until I heard

the click of the door in the morning, signaling Dennis's exit for work. I waited a few minutes and then popped out of bed with one goal: speaking to Troy.

I once again removed the strip of paper from my shoe and dialed the number. Someone picked up on the second ring, and a charge of excitement rushed through me.

"Hello, may I please speak with Troy Strum?" I asked, with as much confidence as I could muster.

"Is this an emergency?"

I briefly considered lying, in hopes of getting through, but I didn't want to jeopardize future contact. "No, but it's important that I speak to him as soon as possible."

"I see. This is actually the call center for Sunrise Ranch. They'll start answering calls at eight o'clock in the morning."

"Oh, I forgot. I'm in Europe and the time difference slipped my mind. What time is it there?"

"Eleven PM."

"OK, I'll call back later."

I hung up in exasperation. With everything else on my mind, I'd completely forgotten about the nine-hour time difference. That meant that I had at least nine hours to kill. And then something else I'd forgotten about came to mind—today was the day I was supposed to meet up with Miriam for the canal ride.

I couldn't think of a better way to bide my time.

The day promised to be cold yet clear, but I'd learned in my short time in the country that a clear sky could quickly fill with dark fluff that would spill white fluff. The train ride passed quickly thanks to my preoccupation with all the unrest in my life.

Miriam approached me where I waited, near the ticket booth at the dock.

"My, you are quite colorful today!" she said. "I like the statement."

I looked at myself only to find I was wearing a caramel-colored jacket, a blue sweater, plaid wool pants, a red scarf, a dark-green hat, and purple gloves. I had no recollection of putting any of this on. Clearly, I'd been preoccupied when I got dressed as well. I'd just wanted to get away as fast as possible. Away from Dennis and the suit that wasn't at the cleaners. Away from the bed that held two loveless bodies each night. Away from the lies that he'd continue to spill for as long as I was with him.

I cleared my throat and smiled weakly. "Oh my, you're right. I'm not very coordinated."

"Or you are on the brink of starting a new fashion trend," she said, with that disarming smile. The warmth of it made me want to cry.

"Well come on then. Amsterdam is your oyster! I believe that is what you say in America."

"I hate oysters," I replied, unfamiliar with the phrase.

"It means you can do anything you wish or go anywhere you want in Amsterdam. At least, that is how one of my clients explained the phrase to me."

"Well, I guess I need to change my way of thinking then." I smiled another weak smile.

"At least about oysters." She patted my back, and after she'd paid for our tickets, she directed me to the waiting vessel.

We boarded the canal boat and found two seats toward the front, and as soon as the vessel left the dock, Miriam stepped into the shoes of tour guide, pointing out important buildings and identifying landmarks. A recorded voice coming through a loudspeaker indicated points of interest, but I preferred Miriam's descriptions. We were sheltered from the cold under a curved glass roof, and from the boat, the city seemed even more picturesque. On a normal day, I would have been in heaven cruising along, passing under brick bridges that arched just high enough to allow us to pass. But my mind was heavy with thoughts that were taking a toll on my ability to enjoy myself.

"Get your phone ready, Beth," Miriam said. "See the white drawbridge?"

I nodded.

"Just after we pass it, you'll be able to look down the canal to the left and see almost a dozen bridge arches in a row. It's quite an architectural feat. Really a sight. Every time I go for a boat ride, I take a photo from this vantage point." She slipped off her gloves and held up her phone. "Let's see who gets the best picture."

I laughed wryly. "Well, you will, because I don't have a phone." I'd never thought about it before, but now I wondered if this was yet another way Dennis kept my world small and controlled.

"Wow, Beth from California, you are full of surprises. I do not think I have met anyone your age without a phone. You must be very happy to live in the present." She smiled and then moved to the other side of the boat to snap her photo. "I think I got a good one," she said, coming back. "The picture always changes based on the weather and the sun. Kind of like life." She grinned.

"Yes, weather is a big deal here, I'm learning. In California, we don't have to deal with too much variation. The sun is usually out and there's rarely a need for hats and gloves unless you go to the mountains and ski."

"Sounds predictable. Do you ski, Beth?" she asked, sitting back down beside me.

"I used to ski when I was younger," I said with a nod. "I joined the ski club in high school so that I could learn." I didn't tell her that the club paid for all the rental expenses so that the sport would be affordable for everyone. I looked at her and found her looking back at me as if my story about skiing was the most interesting one in the world. It caught me off guard. "And you? Do you ski?"

She laughed. "Oh no. First of all, I came from a very poor town that wasn't near mountains. And second of all, look around you. The Netherlands is as flat as it gets." She continued looking at me. "Tell me, Beth from California, what line of work are you in? I have you pegged as an office girl. Am I right?"

I felt a pang of shame. Would she look down on me for not working? I laughed to myself. I couldn't believe I was worrying about what a prostitute might think about how I lived my life.

"I worked in an office briefly, years ago. That's where I met my husband."

"I see. And now?" she asked with a smile. "What kind

of work do you do?"

"I stayed home to raise our son."

I felt the knot in my chest tighten.

"Oh, lovely, and how old is your son?"

"Sixteen."

She must have noticed the tears filling my eyes because she steered the conversation in a different direction. "Wow, then I am way off on your age! I am not sure, by my calculations, that you would be old enough to have a sixteen-year-old. I put you at maybe twenty-nine or thirty, but that would mean you gave birth at twelve and that is not possible."

It was my turn to laugh. Twenty-nine! How could she possibly think that? I shook my head. "That is the nicest thing anyone has said to me, ever. I'm actually thirty-eight."

"That is a shock. You must come from good stock! You are so fit and present yourself so naturally that you misled me. No makeup, just natural beauty. Usually, I am very good at guessing people's ages."

Noticing that the canal boat was approaching the dock again, I swallowed a lump of sadness. I wished we could keep going around and around, so that I'd never have to step back into reality. Before anxiety could take hold, I quickly asked,

"Do you know of a place we can go and have stamppot?"

"Ha! You are a funny one, Beth. Of course. Are you up for a bit of a walk or would you like to catch a tram?"

"Let's walk."

As we made our way through the city, I lost track of the weather, the time, and my surroundings and focused on our conversation about the bike rules on the road. Miriam was so easy to talk to. When we got to the restaurant she had in mind, she was greeted by name and immediately seated at a window table that overlooked the canal.

"This place is known for its stamppot," she said, not looking up from her menu. "Where did you learn about this dish?"

"I had it at the hotel we were staying at, but I'm certain this will be a lot better.

How did you manage this?" I asked, motioning to our table, the best in the place, and the crowd huddled inside the front door, waiting to be seated.

"Let's just say that I know the owner." She winked at me impishly.

Sure enough, when the food came, it was clear that the cook at the hotel must have cooked too many hamburgers and not enough stamppot. That stamppot didn't hold a candle to the one I was eating.

Voices filled the room at a loud volume, but Miriam had the power to make everything else fade into the background.

"So tell me more about your son," she said gently.

"I wish I could!" shot out of me, and then I felt my eyes fill with tears again. I looked out the window to settle myself, and when I finally looked back at Miriam, her eyes held a look of warmth and openness. Before I knew it, I was telling her all about his love of LEGO and his fear of goats; about how I'd had him at twenty-two and had wanted to have another child. I never mentioned Dennis by name, but he was ever present in the conversation.

My monologue soon ground to a halt. I couldn't put into words the current situation. Perhaps because I didn't fully understand it myself.

"So he is at home?"

With that, something inside of me snapped. Not only did my tears fall freely—I slipped my sunglasses on because I was beyond trying to contain them—my words did too. I told Miriam about the mysterious accident and about how I wasn't allowed to see Troy, and why.

Miriam listened intently, her hand periodically touching mine in a comforting way. Finally, I revealed what had happened just that morning. A month of pain, sadness, anxiety, and longing had poured out of me, and I was left feeling spent. And calm.

As if reading my mind, she said, "You must feel a little lighter now. That was a lot to carry around with you."

"You're right. I don't have anyone to talk to about it. Thank you. I'm afraid I've ruined our outing. I swear I didn't mean for this to happen."

"It needed to come out and I am glad to be here to receive it. I could tell in the café the other day that you could use a friend."

"Really? How?" I hadn't realized I was so transparent.

"Let's just say, in my profession, you learn to read social cues and then some." She smiled and patted my hand.

It was the first time in years that I'd been able to talk about tough things without being shut down or told to appreciate what I had. She didn't know Dennis or have any prior knowledge of our life. She passed no judgment. She just listened.

I was overwhelmed by her kindness and her presence.

Our server came by with the peppermint teas Miriam had ordered earlier. I sat back, removed my sunglasses, and breathed deeply.

"Sounds like you need to do some investigating," Miriam said to me once the server had left. "Perhaps there's a paper trail of some sort that will help you. Where does your husband keep his papers? Does he have a briefcase? That might be a good place to start." She pointed a finger at me to emphasize the idea.

"Yes, I need to do that." I took a sip of the tea and let it calm me further. "I also need to catch the four o'clock train so that I can make that call and hopefully talk to Troy."

She glanced at her watch. "That may be difficult. The train leaves in ten minutes, and we are farther than fifteen minutes from the station." An idea seemed to come to her. "But, you know, you could use my phone. I know a quiet place where you can make your call and won't be interrupted. You won't have to worry about your husband walking in."

"Are you sure? It's an international call. It might be expensive."

"Why don't you see if you get through first."

After finishing our tea and settling up the bill, we headed out into the afternoon. Daylight was fleeting in the winter in Amsterdam, and the yellow glow of a low sun held no warmth, which kept us moving.

Soon, I recognized my surroundings, and I had an idea of where this "quiet place" might be. Sure enough, minutes later we were outside Miriam's window in the Red Light District.

"I usually don't come here on my time off, but it is the closest option for privacy and quiet. My home is farther away, or I would have offered that."

So she didn't live here after all.

I felt an odd sense of normalcy as we slipped into her window. She pulled the heavy red curtain closed, and I took a minute to scan the small room. There was a bed covered with a burgundy velvet blanket and a mirror that extended the entire length of the wall it was set against. There was a sink with several soap pumps, and beside an alarm button on the wall was a list of rules. I was interested in reading them but figured that might be rude. I wasn't there to educate myself on the protocols of prostitution. In the center of the room was a table on which sat a vase with flowers (I knew where those had come from!). The room was lit in a red hue that gave it the feeling of a bordello I'd seen in a movie, but when Miriam switched on the white light, it looked like a dorm room I'd visited when I toured the local college campus in high school.

"OK, you can make your call now, in peace and quiet." Miriam handed me her phone and then added, "You can sit on the bed. It is clean and tidy."

"Can you help me dial the number?" I asked. "I don't own a cell phone and I don't want to screw it up." I looked at her and felt pathetic, but she just smiled and took the phone back.

"Do you want me to wait outside?"

"No, I'd actually love it if you stayed."

Her presence gave me confidence and strength.

She nodded and dialed the number as I recited it by memory. Then she handed the phone to me again and patted the bed, indicating I should sit. I did, and she sat beside me. I heard clicks and then a buzzing instead of a ringing. On the fourth buzz, someone picked up.

"Sunrise Ranch, how may I direct your call?"

"I'd like to speak with Troy Strum. This is his mother, Beth—"

The line went dead with a click.

"See!" I cried, frustration threatening to overwhelm me. "I can't get further than this. Why do they hang up? Why are we disconnected?"

Miriam was frowning. "That is curious. Something does not seem right about this whole thing. If I were you, I would start with your husband's briefcase. See if you can find anything related to your son. It might just be a coincidence or a bad connection. I would also suggest not giving your name and not saying you are his mother. Anonymity might be better at this point."

More than anything, I wanted to believe it was just a coincidence, but I felt in my gut that this wasn't the case. I needed to get some answers.

Miriam insisted that I return the next day at one o'clock, wanting to make sure I was OK. I'd never had a person care so much about my well-being. When we left her window, a couple of people gave us looks, but I was way beyond caring. She walked me to the train station and hugged me before heading home. "Don't worry, Beth from California. Tomorrow will be better."

"I apologize for ending our afternoon on such a low note," I said. "I really didn't have any plans to unleash all my personal issues on you."

"You have nothing to apologize for. I am honored that you shared your story. Everyone needs someone to listen. Today, I was that person for you. Perhaps you will repay the favor in the future."

I hoped that I could. "You've been a good friend to me. And I really enjoyed our canal ride!"

"Me too. Like you Americans say, it was a blast!" She smiled and winked.

"Doo eee," I offered.

"Doei," she replied. "You catch on quick!"

I watched her silhouette disappear into the mass of people and felt so grateful to have crossed paths with her.

As I sat on the train, listening to the clicking of the rails, I thought about finding Sunrise Ranch and confronting Troy. I thought about finding the hospital Troy had been taken to and interrogating the staff. I thought about confronting my husband about my son's whereabouts. I thought about calling my mother. These were all actions I could take, but where would they get me? Every scenario required trust, and at this point, I didn't know if I could trust anyone.

When I arrived at the hotel, Dennis was already there, and in a foul mood. There was talk that the merger would be pushed into the new year. With Christmas approaching, momentum had been lost, and Dennis was finding it impossible to get the "Dutchies" to respond. I was sure he'd already calculated the bonus and raise he'd get for being part of this deal.

"What does that mean for us?" I asked, hanging up my coat. This was good news for me. Going home would be the best next step, even if I didn't know what the steps after that looked like.

"I'll know for sure tomorrow," he said, looking out the window, "but I think we may head back to the US in a few days."

"That sounds great."

He turned to me. "Why does that sound great?" he snapped. "I thought you liked being here?"

"I just can't imagine a Christmas without Troy. If we're back, we can do what it takes to spend it together," I said firmly.

"How dense is it inside of that brain of yours?" he said, his voice rising. "How many times have I told you that he isn't coming back to you? How many times have I told you to let go?"

I swallowed. "I don't understand how you can expect me to let him go," I said, trying to maintain my cool. "He's my only son. He's a part of me." I felt the tears return and was surprised I had any more to shed.

"Going home isn't going to change the fact that Troy is in a better place—away from you and all your doting and coddling. He is where he is because of you, Beth. Leave it alone."

I wasn't sure if it was a result of letting it all out to Miriam earlier, but a rage I had no idea I possessed burst out of me, and I did the unthinkable. I lunged toward Dennis and threw my fists into his chest. "You can't keep me from my son!" I screamed. "He needs me, and I need him!" I kept beating his chest as sobs replaced my anger. "Where is he? You have to tell me. Where is he?"

Dennis pushed me away, down to the bed. I continued to sob, and when I looked up moments later, his eyes were cold and still. He brushed the front of his shirt a few times, as if he were trying to rid himself of lint. "I'm going downstairs for a drink. You need to get a grip on yourself. Do not follow me. I need a break from your madness."

With that, he turned and left.

I collapsed backward on the bed and stared at the ceiling. In all the years we'd been married, I'd never lost it like that. I'd never questioned Dennis. He had me under his thumb. He always had the last word. He held all the power: power over me, over Troy, over our family, over our life.

In my head, I heard King Lear's words to his daughter: *"Nothing will come of nothing."*

But something could come from something. It was my move.

You're the one who has to change, to act, I reminded myself.

Remembering Miriam's suggestion, I immediately stood and scanned the room for Dennis's briefcase. He usually locked it in the closet safe, but there it was, propped against the legs of the desk. He must have gotten to the room just before I had and then forgotten about it after the fight.

I grabbed it, sat on the floor, and began rifling through its contents. Spreadsheets and data sheets were in the first pocket. In the second pocket were files and portfolio papers. One zipped pocket held a Dutch dictionary and a map of Rotterdam. The other zipped pocket had Dutch PR ads for WTS. In that pocket, there was a section secured with Velcro. I stuck my hand in and pulled out a piece of paper. My heart leaped into my throat when I saw the letterhead: *Sunrise Ranch*.

It took me a moment to realize what I was looking at—a one-page admittance form. Sunrise Ranch was a drug-rehabilitation facility. There were handwritten notes in the margins. This was a photocopy of the original.

I read it quickly. Troy had been admitted one week after his accident. His stay would be six months, minimum, and his case was being further reviewed at the juvenile court since he was under legal age. I felt as if I were reading facts about a stranger.

There was a case number and personal information about Troy. Parental info and address. There were yes/no questions about school district he attended. All the info matched up until I got to the affidavit section where there was a written account of the accident and that is when it all went upside down. I read it in its entirety, but it stayed with me in phrases that burned into my brain.

Under the influence of alcohol/prescription drugs
Unable to communicate clearly
Driving while under the influence of alcohol and oxycodone

and crashing into the car of an elderly woman,
causing severe injuries to her
possession of prescription drugs
and proof of dealing drugs
endangerment of life...

I blinked. Troy. My son. Dependent on alcohol and oxycodone? Dealing drugs? How could that be? This couldn't be true.

I looked back at the form and read the notes in the margin.

Mother has a history of alcohol addiction.

Mother has been jailed for dealing oxycodone and other methamphetamines.

Mother can be a danger to her son.

Recommend no contact with mother.

Now I knew this was a mistake. Someone had gotten the paperwork mixed up.

I sat there on the floor for a moment, dumbfounded, before hurriedly placing the admittance form back where I'd found it. Then I reconsidered, folded up the paper, and slipped it in the zippered pocket of my purse.

It's all just been a big mistake, I repeated to myself. *Just a big mistake.*

17

Bad Contact

I didn't sleep much that night as the gravity—and reality—of the situation began to sink in. Dennis had lied to the rehab facility. I barely drank at social events, and the only medication I took was over-the-counter flu medicine on the rare occasions I got sick.

I wished I had some of that medicine now. I felt sick to my stomach. Sick over the dishonesty and sick that I hadn't known that our son was in trouble. How could anyone sleep when they'd been falsely accused of things that were keeping them from their child?

Days before his accident, Troy had been helping me replace a light bulb in the kitchen when "Angie," by the Rolling Stones, came on the radio. He started playing air guitar and I joined in with air drums and we laughed as we mutilated the song. How could I be a danger to my son?

My life had officially gone from sad to spiraling out of control.

One thing was for sure: I wasn't going to get any real answers from Dennis. The next day, I'd go to Amsterdam and tell Miriam about what I'd found and hopefully get in touch with Troy. That was as far ahead as I could plan.

When morning finally came, I got up and noticed that Dennis's briefcase was gone, as was his brown suit. He must have returned to our room late and left early, during one of the brief periods I'd been sleeping.

I immediately called Sunrise Ranch, but the call center answered so I hung up. Needing to get out of the hotel, I decided to take an earlier train and just walk around and maybe get a sausage at the Christmas market. I wasn't meeting Miriam until one o'clock.

The little world that I'd created for myself in Amsterdam, a small rectangle of the inner city marked by four points—the train station, the museums, the Christmas market, and the Oude Kerk—was my safe haven. I'd made my way within the confines of this rectangle successfully each time I visited, and I'd done so alone. I knew where to eat, where to buy flowers, where to see art, where to watch ice skaters, where to buy porcelain, where to catch a canal boat and a train. I knew where to buy cheese and fifty-year-old whiskey and magic mushrooms. I even knew where Anne Frank used to live. And, oddly enough, the Red Light District was part of my refuge. It gave me a sense of comfort, regardless of what was happening behind the glass windows and doors.

When I arrived at the Christmas market, the vendors

were just opening their stalls and spreading out their wares for display. The sausage wheel had already been loaded, but the meat still needed time to cook so I meandered away from the market, grateful for the weather that offered no extremes—no rain, no wind, no snow. I walked down a pedestrian road where stores were already open.

I thought about how Dennis had said that we'd be leaving in a few days. Did this even matter now? He'd kept me from Troy for a month. Why would things change? *I have to get a hold of Troy*, I thought, tears stinging my eyes. That was my only hope. He would tell me where he was, he would tell me exactly where and I'd go to him. This plan settled me enough to keep moving, and I returned to the sausage stand in time to be their first customer.

I stood at the wooden counter that was usually impossible to belly up to and ate the sausage with a vengeance, reminded of the fact that I hadn't eaten dinner the previous night.

"Hoi."

I looked up and noticed an attractive man behind the counter smiling at me. He was dressed in black and wore one of those pincushion hats.

"Hoi." I smiled back.

"You could be our public-relations manager. Just watching you eat that sausage made me want to eat one myself, and I'm around them every day." He winked at me, bringing my attention to his blue eyes. His sandy-brown hair stuck out of his hat, and I couldn't decide if he looked more like Brad Pitt or Leonardo DiCaprio. Regardless, he was handsome—and definitely younger than I was.

"I don't think you need a PR person. Every time I come here, it's so crowded."

"Ah, you are a repeat customer? How is it that I have not seen that beautiful face before?" He grinned, and I immediately felt awkward. I had no practice when it came to flirting. And why would anyone want to flirt with me anyway?

"This is a busy place," I said, with a small smile. "I'm sure you have no time to look up." I took another bite.

"I would welcome a glance at a beautiful woman like you." He reached over and offered me a napkin then pointed to his chin. "You have a little mustard there."

"Oh, thank you," I said, feeling silly, but he just looked at me with his blue eyes, a welcome distraction from my self-consciousness.

"Where are you from?" He stepped back and spun the sausage wheel with just enough force to shift the sausages down, closer to the grate.

"California."

"I have heard that song 'California Girls'!" He held up his spatula like a microphone and sang a couple of lines in a comical tone. "They are right about what they sing."

I blushed. "You're so kind," I said, and immediately regretted it. I sounded like an old woman. Truly, I was out of my league but flattered to be engaged in a playful conversation like this.

"Hoi, Luke." One of the older men in the booth said something to the guy in Dutch. With a start, I noticed a line had formed and the counter was filling up. In the short time we'd been talking, half of Amsterdam had arrived. I finished my sausage and glanced over at Luke, who was now helping customers. He caught my gaze and dipped his head in a farewell nod.

I didn't want to leave. I wanted to stay at that counter and flirt. No one had spoken to me that way since I got married. Especially not my husband.

Glancing at my watch, I realized I still had time and decided to walk some more. The driver who'd taken Dennis and me to Rotterdam had told me that Amsterdam had a modern part, but I had no interest in widening my surroundings. The knowledge that I was going home in a few days had me soaking up the scenery in my rectangle of security. I noticed every facade of every building and every arch of every canal bridge. I noticed how the sun was like a spotlight. When it penetrated the gaps in the buildings, it illuminated swatches of life. In minutes, the light would change and something new would be illuminated. The details in the brick wall would fade and the ripples on the canal waters would be accentuated as boats went by.

I saw her from a distance, her back to me, her hair bouncing on her shoulders as she approached our meeting spot. Again, I was struck by how confident she looked, how established. How could she be someone who stood in a window and sold herself? How could she be a prostitute? Yesterday, I'd spilled my heart out to her, and she'd treated me with such empathy and compassion. How could she lie with men for money? The whole thing had me baffled.

"Hello, Miriam," I called, as I came up behind her.

She turned around. "Oh, I was expecting you to come from the other direction."

"I got here early and had time to kill, so I went to the Christmas market and had a sausage roll. They're my favorite."

She grinned. "You are more of a local than I gave you credit for! Those are some of the best eats around, and they go away after Christmas—but maybe that is why we love them so much. We cannot take them for granted!"

"Maybe you're right." I thought about Luke. Was he a local or a traveling sausage man?

"So how are you, Beth from California? You seem to have some color in your cheeks."

I cleared my throat as my reality hit me with full force, Luke's attention immediately forgotten. "Well, I checked my husband's briefcase, like you suggested, and found out where my son is . . . but it doesn't seem real." My son. Abusing alcohol? Addicted to pills? I wasn't feeling ready to disclose this to Miriam. That would mean that I believed it. "Where shall we go?"

"Well, you've already had a sausage, so you probably don't want to eat more?" She glanced at me, and I nodded. "How about a cup of tea, or do you want to walk?"

"Let's walk."

She led me away from my rectangle, and we ended up parallel to a canal in a residential area. This canal was quiet but large enough to allow boats to moor on either side.

"Do people live on those?" I asked, noticing small garden boxes and outdoor furniture on some of the boats.

"Oh yes, it's very common, given the cost of housing in the city, but I believe most of the occupants would choose to live on a boat no matter what. It's in their blood."

"Why do you say that?"

"The Netherlands has spent most of its history reclaiming land from the sea. Houseboats are a byproduct of this struggle for balance."

I nodded. "This is the second time I'm hearing about the country's battle with the sea."

Some of the boats were large and had flat tops that provided space for patio furniture, plants, BBQs, and bike storage. Others looked like traditional sailboats, big enough to contain living quarters and galleys. That life seemed romantic.

"Have you ever wanted to live on a houseboat?" I asked Miriam with a smile. "They look so quaint."

"I like having my feet on solid ground," she said. "It used to be for poor people—a lot of artists lived on boats. There are over two thousand houseboats in Amsterdam now." She gestured to one up ahead. "Some of these houseboats are really upscale. Prices have gone up close to 40 percent in the last five years. The price increase comes from the value of the berth, not the boat itself. But look at this one."

We approached a beautiful houseboat and Miriam encouraged me to look into its massive front window, which offered a view of a baby grand piano and large, comfortable furniture. "Not too shabby, huh? This was converted from a World War II munitions boat. The Dutch are famous for their resourcefulness."

On the front deck, hanging from a metal boom, was a set of swings dangling in the breeze, lying in wait. The thought of children pumping their legs to swing across the deck and over the water made me grin.

"There's so much to learn about this city!" I said. "You know so much."

"Well, I have been here for a decade. You get to know your surroundings. Amsterdam rescued me . . ." She left the comment hanging like a forgotten sock on a clothesline. But before I could prompt her to continue, she stopped and gestured to a doorway. "Care to have a cup of tea at my flat?"

I raised my eyebrows in surprise but nodded. The brick facade looked like many I'd seen. The windows had red shutters, and on the lower ones were window boxes filled with red, gold, and silver ornaments and small green, fir tree branches, taking the place of plants that couldn't survive the frigid winter. The door was wooden, and something resembling a family crest or shield was carved in it.

"Is that symbolic of something?" I asked, gesturing to the carving as Miriam unlocked the door.

"Not that I know of, but I liked the look of it." She smiled. "After you."

Everything about her flat was unexpected. Lace curtains hung in the front windows. The furniture was eclectic but worked in the space. A floor-to-ceiling bookshelf spanned one wall, and it was filled with books and decorated with strings of lights intertwined with branches of greenery and berries. A small Christmas tree stood in the main window. Miriam directed me to take off my coat and sit down while she made some tea. I draped my coat over the comfy looking chair with an ottoman nearest the door and looked around.

Most of her books were in Dutch, but I spotted a grief-counseling book in English, along with a copy of *The Dinner*, by Herman Koch, and a book about Vermeer. I paged through the art book but did not see any tulips. Also on the bookshelf was a black-and-white photograph of a family. Hers? I leaned closer to examine it. There was a man and a woman and three girls. Miriam appeared to be the oldest of the three, but the picture had clearly been taken quite a while ago. The girl next to her looked quite a bit younger and the smallest girl clung to the woman's leg, looking down. No one was smiling. Miriam's wide eyes in the photo transfixed me. There was something about her look: maybe shyness, maybe uncertainty. Perhaps the photographer had caught her by surprise?

"Is this your family?" I asked, when she entered the living room with a tray that held a blue-and-white teapot and two cups and saucers.

"It is," she said quietly.

"How old are you in that picture?"

She set the tray on the coffee table then sat back on the couch, seemingly deep in thought. I took a seat in the chair across from her.

"I am sorry. What did you ask me?" She looked at me with an expression that suggested she'd just realized where she was.

"I wondered how old you were in that family photo."

"Eleven," she said, leaning forward. She lifted the tea

bag from the pot then dunked it a few times before pouring the liquid into the cups.

"When did your family move here?" I asked, standing to retrieve a cup then settling into the chair again.

Miriam's forehead was furrowed as she reached for her cup. Her unease seemed to grow, but she smiled briefly.

"I left home about four years after that picture was taken, and I have not seen my family since." She nodded as if agreeing with herself then took a sip of tea.

"Oh . . . that must be hard." I wanted to ask her why but didn't know how to go about it, so I asked the next logical question to break the awkward silence. "How did you end up in Amsterdam?"

Had she come here to be a prostitute?

"I came here with my ex-boyfriend. He brought me here."

"Do you miss your family?" I asked. My heart clenched as Troy's face filled my mind.

"No." She sipped some more tea.

"I cannot imagine . . ."

"No, you cannot imagine what I left behind," she replied. "It is not something to miss, that is for sure."

"Do you ever talk to your family?" I said, my own discomfort growing. I sincerely wanted to hear about her past, but I didn't want to make her feel uncomfortable, especially in her own home.

"No. Some things need to be left behind, for the sake of survival."

I shook my head slightly. "I don't really understand."

"No one can, really. It is not something people want to hear about."

"I would. I mean, I would want to hear about it if you were willing to share," I offered.

"I have not shared my story with anyone except my ex-boyfriend."

"Well, I haven't shared my story with anyone but you," I said, looking at her encouragingly. "Where did you grow up?"

She sat back and regarded me. Assessing whether I was worthy of what she was about to share? Or whether she wanted to divulge intimate details about her past to a stranger? To me, Miriam didn't feel like a stranger. I felt closer to her than I did to anyone in my life right now, despite having known her for less than a week.

"I grew up in a small rural town to the east."

"Where?"

"Romania. The town was centered on drilling for oil and natural gas, and the countryside was as barren as the people. Not many trees or greenery. I remember everyone always being cold and hungry. We lived in a dark house that my mother kept tidy, but it never looked clean. My dad worked in an oil field miles from our home and my mother raised us girls." She paused and glanced out the window behind me. "I am pretty sure I have more siblings now."

"Why do you say that?"

"Let's just say that there was not much to do in my hometown, and that is one way to stay warm."

"Hmm." I nodded and noticed that she hadn't touched

her tea for a while, so I leaned over and offered her a refill, to heat it up. She accepted it and took a sip. I refilled my cup as well.

"Every Friday and Saturday, my dad went to the pub in town with his pockets full and returned home with his pockets empty. He'd play cards and dice with other men from the oil field, and most of the time, he gambled away what money he made. My mom would often send me to fetch him before he lost the house." She closed her eyes for a moment. "The pub was smoky and full of loud voices, and when we walked home, my father always had a conversation with himself about how Mr. Menlin had cheated, or how Mr. Radu's luck never ran out. I would walk behind him quietly, feeling disappointed that there would be no bread or meat anytime soon. My mother tried her best to keep us fed, and she did what she could to stretch what little food we had. She many times offered to do mending for the neighbor in exchange for a few eggs or biscuits.

"When I was old enough, I attended school, and she walked me there each morning. This guaranteed me a snack that usually served as my lunch."

"You have kind memories of your mother," I said, but she was quick to correct me.

"My memories of home do not include memories of kindness."

"I'm sorry. Please, go on."

She took a sip and gazed toward the window behind me again as she spoke. "One day my father called me into the kitchen and told me that I needed to go to the home of

Mr. Radu directly after school. He was the butcher in town, so I hoped that my father had won some meat. But he told me that Mr. Radu needed some help and that I was to do whatever he asked of me. I assumed I would be paying off a gambling debt by cleaning or cooking for Mr. Radu. Even though I was only eleven, I had a good working knowledge of the kitchen and lots of practice making beds and cleaning floors and bathrooms." She blinked and swallowed. "But when I got to Mr. Radu's house, I found out that he didn't want me to clean or cook."

"I don't understand."

"Of course you don't. No one could understand a father sending his eleven-year-old daughter to pay off a debt because of a filthy gambling and drinking habit that was more important than keeping his daughter safe." She glanced at the photo. "Whenever I start to miss family, I look at that photo to remind me of what I left behind."

My heart broke for Miriam. "I don't know what to say. Did Mr. Radu hurt you?"

She continued looking at the window. "At first, he aroused himself by exploring my very young and immature body. He would run his hands under my shirt or over my behind and would then excuse himself to finish his 'business' in the bathroom." Her lip curled in disgust. "But eventually, that was not enough. He raped me two days before I turned twelve."

I felt bile rise into my throat and choked it down. "Oh my god, Miriam, I am so sorry. Did your mother know?"

"At first, no," she said, taking another sip of tea. "I told my father I didn't want to go anymore, after the first visit, and he got angry and hit me. He told me that we all did our part to help the family and that that was my part. Mr. Radu would give me a piece of smoked jerky afterwards, like a reward, and the sad thing was that I was so hungry, I accepted it gratefully. Finally, I went to my mother and begged her to talk to my father, but she had no power. She had no interest, it seemed, in advocating for me. She told me to stop complaining, that we all had to carry the burdens of the family.

"When I was fifteen, I met a boy at school, and we quickly became sexually active. I thought that was a normal thing to do. Eventually, I told him about Mr. Radu, and he didn't like the idea of sharing me. He promised to take me away when he'd saved enough money, and I was blinded by the promise of freedom and by his desire to have me to himself. With him, I felt like I belonged somewhere. The summer I turned sixteen, I got on the back of his motorcycle, and we headed west. I never said goodbye to my parents or my sisters. I can't bear to think that Katia might have had to take my place with Mr. Radu, but I had to save myself."

I shook my head. "That must have been so hard, leaving your family behind."

"There was no other option. My father was spineless and had already written me off as damaged goods because of his own deficits. In our town, prostitution was a byproduct of the large number of transient oil workers. That was where I was heading if I didn't get out of there. My boyfriend and I camped along the road that summer and drove all the way to Amsterdam, where he had a cousin, Franco. What I didn't realize was that the cousin was a drug dealer. My boyfriend became addicted to heroin not long after we arrived, and I became collateral for his drug fix, so I went from Mr. Radu to Franco. I had no way out. My boyfriend became violent when he was high, and he started beating me up. The heroin fried his brain."

I was having a hard enough time digesting the idea that my son might be abusing alcohol and oxycodone. Miriam's story was totally out of my realm of comprehension. I could only shake my head in disbelief.

"When I stood up to him and told him I didn't want to be his whore, he threw me out and I stayed on the street for three days. I wandered around and looked for warm places, out of the wind, where I could sleep. I refused to beg or to sell myself for money. Three days. That is how long I lasted before I begged to come back."

"My god, Miriam," I said, tears filling my eyes. "When I look at you, I see such a strong woman."

"I became a strong woman because of my past," she said firmly. "For a while, my boyfriend passed me around to pay for his drugs, until I became legal and then he forced me, through a friend's connection, to enter De Wallen, the Red Light District as a sex worker. It was actually better than being passed around—I finally had a say in what I did. The Red Light District actually saved my life. It has rules and controls. Before, anyone could sexually abuse me if my boyfriend said it was OK. Now, I could call the shots. He wasn't allowed to be around to see if I accepted or rejected a customer. He wasn't around when I refused certain sexual scenarios. But he was around when I came home, and he quickly cleaned my pockets of all my cash."

"All of this is so hard to believe," I said, feeling the weight of my ignorance. "What happened to your boyfriend? I can't imagine you're still with him?"

"I began trying to hide money before he took it all from me, but he caught me putting cash in my boot one time and beat me with his belt so bad that I couldn't work for several days. He was mean. The drugs had killed his soul and all that was left was a shell of a person who lived for his next high. I used to pray to God to help me out of the mess I was in, and one day he answered.

"I got the call from Franco—my boyfriend had been driving over one hundred miles per hour on his motorcycle on the autobahn, high on heroin, when he crashed headfirst into the cement overpass support. He was killed instantly. That part made me sad. I would have liked for him to suffer." She shook her head and grimaced.

I hadn't realized I'd been leaning forward. I leaned back and exhaled at the same time as Miriam looked up and met my gaze.

"Yep, that is how I ended up in Amsterdam."

"How long ago was your boyfriend's accident?"

"Ten years."

"And you're still—" I stopped, but she finished the sentence.

"I am still a prostitute, by choice, and live a very calm and safe life. I make my own choices, I own a flat, I attend the opera, I have male suitors, and I never want for food or money. I am pretty good at my job," she said with a wink, "and my life is my own and it is a good one. All I want is a stable life where I make my own decisions. Do you think that is odd?"

"I guess I'm not sure what I think. I can't really have an opinion about something I know nothing about. And look at me," I said, scoffing. "I haven't had sex for close to seventeen years. That must be a crime somewhere."

We looked at each other and burst into laughter, defusing the serious charge in the room. In fact, we laughed so hard that I thought I might spill my tea. When our giggles finally died out, I looked at her and asked, "So if you wanted to walk away from the Red Light District, you could?"

"Yes, I could, but prostitution is what I know. It's been a part of my life since I was eleven. I now know how to navigate my life so that I am in charge. No one will ever tell me what to do. There is a power in the system that I now own. I know many people would find my choices horrific, but no one has lived my life. No one has walked in my shoes. It is none of their business to worry about me."

I nodded. "I never thought of it that way. I have to say, the day I met you, I made certain assumptions. The next time I saw you, in the window, I had trouble understanding how you could have a foot in that world. I now see why." I got up, put my teacup down, and went over to the couch to hug her. "Thank you for honoring me with your story. You are, what we say in America, a survivor."

She hugged me back. "And you, Beth from California,

are a good friend. Thank you for not judging me. I have kept my story tucked away because I have always feared that if I spoke of it, it would come back to life."

"I promise you that I have nothing but admiration for you and what you stand for," I said, pulling away and perching next to her on the couch.

"You realize that you are saying that prostitution is OK? You seemed to have a different opinion when I first met you."

"How do you know?"

"Like I said, in this profession, you become really good at reading people. When I saw you looking at the statue imbedded in the cobblestones, you had a look of disapproval on your face."

My jaw dropped a little. "I'm sorry. I always thought I'd be the last person to find fault in others' choices." Given that I grew up in an unconventional family setting, I never had an interest in comparing myself to others. I would be forced to confront my own lack of a father or siblings. But Miriam's life scenario was next level, tragic.

"So will I be seeing you wear one of those T-shirts that say *Prostitutes' Lives Matter*?"

I laughed. "Maybe not quite yet. But who knows."

She laughed with me, and then we carried our dishes into the kitchen and she showed me the rest of the place. It had a master bedroom and a tiny second room with a day bed, a nightstand, and a desk. The bathroom was between the two. The flat was the perfect size. It was her sanctuary.

"Well," she said, leading me back to the living room, "I really had no intention of going into a dissertation about my childhood. What I really want to hear about is what you found out."

I retrieved my purse from beside the chair, and we both sat down on the couch. I dug out the admittance form and handed it to Miriam.

"My husband and I had a fight when I got back to the hotel. He usually keeps his briefcase locked in the safe, but luckily he stormed out before he had a chance to. I found this deep in a pocket."

She read it over and then gave me a quizzical look. "You did not tell me about your past."

I frowned in confusion then quickly realized what she was referring to. "Oh no, those handwritten notes aren't true! I've never been to jail, I've never done drugs, and I'm not a danger to my child. Dennis must have said those things to keep Troy away from me. I know it sounds unbelievable, but it's true. I have no idea why my husband doesn't want me to have a relationship with our son." I shook my head. "I can only assume it's about control."

"Well, if what you say is true, it seems that your husband is trying to place blame on you so that he can justify the actions of your son and free himself of any responsibility."

Huh. "I'd never thought of that. It's just so far from the truth that I don't know how his word can override mine. I'm Troy's mother."

"Power comes in many shapes and forms," Miriam said, handing the form back to me. "Looks like money is the shape it has taken in this scenario."

Of course. That made sense. Dennis had always used

his money to direct our lives. Why would it be any different now? I had no desire to return to that hotel. I needed to contact Troy, though. If I could talk to him, we could make a plan.

"I wish I didn't have to leave, but I need to catch the four o'clock train back to Rotterdam. I really need to call Troy to see if I can get to the bottom of this."

"You are welcome to use my phone if you'd like. It might be a better idea. If they are blocking your call from the hotel, you may have a better chance getting through from a new number."

"I never thought of that either," I replied, looking at her with bewilderment. I felt so ill-equipped to get through this mess, so naïve. "You wouldn't mind me using your phone? I'll pay for the long-distance cost. With the time difference, it's so hard to make contact, and I have Dennis to circumnavigate."

"Not at all. Find a place you feel comfortable and make the call. I can disappear if you'd like, give you privacy."

"No!" I blurted. The thought of being alone right now was too scary. Her presence would give me a boost of confidence. "Please stay."

"OK."

She handed me her phone, and I dialed the memorized number in haste. Miraculously, someone picked up after two rings.

"Sunrise Ranch, how may I help you?"

"Yes, may I please speak to Troy Strum?"

"I'm sorry, can you say the name again? I'm new here."

My heart sped up. "Troy Strum."

"One moment, please."

As if sensing my nervousness, Miriam took my hand and squeezed it gently. Before I could say anything, I heard a familiar husky voice on the other end of the line.

"Hello?"

I could barely speak, my joy and relief were so great. "Troy, it's Mom. How are you?" I was finally talking to my son. I felt light-headed and full of hope. Finally, I'd find out what had happened and how I could help.

"Who?"

"It's me. Your *mom*. I've missed you so much. Are you OK?"

There was silence on the line.

My heart sped up again. "Troy, are you there?"

"Are you kidding me? Dad told me you wrote me off as your son because I turned out to be just like you—a loser."

My skin went cold. "What are you talking about, Troy? I've been trying to get a hold of you since the day of the accident. I had no idea where you were, and I looked everywhere. Your father told me that the hospital staff wouldn't allow me to visit you." I paused. "You're not a loser, son." My voice was stretched thin, and my face was wet.

"You're pathetic. Dad told me you'd say something like this if you called. How could you not find me? Dad knew where I was. He told me he begged you to come to the hospital, but you refused. He said you were glad to be rid of me and hoped to never see me again. He told me you hated me for hurting that old lady." His voice rose. "It's your fault that I got in that accident because of your past . . ." He made a coughing sound. "Anyway, whatever. No worries. You don't ever have to see me again. Dad said that when I've done my time here, he'll take care of everything."

That hit me like a solid punch to the gut. "My god, Troy! All I want is to see you and to help you. I never said any of those things!"

"Dad told me you'd deny it," he said, disgust in his tone. "Thanks for the bad genes," he said mockingly. "Leave it to you to give me the worst of yourself."

This couldn't be happening. It was surreal. The conversation felt as if it were scripted, straight from a Netflix series about lies and deceit. Still, I had to persevere. Try a different tack. This was my chance to understand what had happened—really happened.

"Troy," I said firmly. "You have got to stop this nonsense. None of what you're saying is true. I've never done drugs or struggled with alcohol, and I haven't written you off. Your father never told me where you were or how I could reach you. You have to believe me."

He laughed loudly. "I have to believe *you*? What a crock. How can you call yourself a mother? How could you just abandon me?" His voice cracked.

My heart was breaking, and I couldn't think fast enough to come up with the right words. What were the right words, after all? *Your father is a liar?*

"I'll come to you. We can spend Christmas together. Please, Troy, I need you."

"I'm beyond needing you. Like I said, Dad will take

care of everything. He told me so. He told me I didn't need your influence in my life. I'm done with this conversation. You're a pathetic mother and I never want to see you again. Do me a favor? Lose this number because I won't answer it again."

The line went dead, and all I heard was a dull buzzing, as if the earth had been unplugged from reality. I looked at Miriam, who was looking at me with sad eyes. "Wow." She rubbed my back.

"I promise you, Miriam, none of what he said is true. I love my son with all my heart." Tears spilled out of my eyes. "It didn't even sound like Troy. Dennis pumped so many lies into him—why? What did I do to deserve this?"

"No one deserves this, Beth. Not you or anyone. This husband of yours sounds like a horrible man and believe me, I have had some experience dealing with horrible men."

That statement stopped me in my tracks. Everyone in my life—my mom, Dennis's colleagues, acquaintances I spent time with occasionally, Troy—they all sang Dennis's praises. They all defended his honor and spewed examples of his generosity, humility, and kindness. Miriam was the first person who could also see what I now saw. No one else would believe me if I told them what was happening. How would I ever get Dennis to be honest with me? I could already see him nonchalantly disregarding my accusations and putting the whole thing on me. The thought of it made bile rise in the back of my throat again.

A sense of helplessness overwhelmed me, and I suddenly felt as if I'd inhaled a hysterical force that had taken me hostage from within. I sobbed so hard I could barely breathe. Miriam just rubbed my back patiently, present, by my side.

A comment Troy had made popped into my head: *He told me you hated me for hurting that old lady.* Dennis had told me she was fine. Another lie. Was anything he'd ever said to me true?

My head throbbed, and my eyes were so swollen I could barely open them. Apparently noticing, Miriam left the room and returned with a warm cloth, which I placed over my eyes. She then scooped up my legs and placed them on the couch. I felt her cover me with an afghan, and I surrendered to her attention, not knowing what to do next.

The thought of going back to the hotel seemed impossible now. But what else could I do? I felt my chest fill with angst and started to weep again. Mercifully, I soon drifted off to the sound of Miriam rooting around in the kitchen.

I awoke to a pleasant aroma. I removed the cloth from my eyes and noticed the light in the room had changed. No sun spilled in through the sheer curtains. Miriam had turned on a lamp that cast soft light into the living room.

"Oh my, what time is it?" I sat up sharply and regretted it. My head still throbbed. I looked into the kitchen but couldn't see Miriam. "I have to go. Dennis will be wondering—"

She stepped into view in the kitchen, her back to me, a dish towel draped over her shoulder. Steam was rising from a pan on the stove and the sizzle of meat and veggies filled the kitchen. She gave the contents of the pan a stir and then wiped her hands on her apron and turned to face me.

"You are not going anywhere until you eat a good meal and plan your next steps. Dennis should be the last thing on your mind right now."

"But—"

"But nothing. You will eat a meal before anything else."

I had to admit the smell was delicious, and my stomach was responding to it with a growl of anticipation, despite how drained I felt.

We settled ourselves at the kitchen table, and I soon learned that Miriam's culinary skills were top-notch. I welcomed the chance to regroup and gain some perspective. We ate in comfortable silence as I devour the contents of the bowl.

"May I have another bowl of this?" I asked, tapping my spoon on my dish. "What is it called? It's so delicious."

"Nasi goreng. It's an Indonesian dish. I'm not sure if you noticed all the Indonesian shops and restaurants around Amsterdam?"

I hadn't. I shook my head.

"Indonesia was a Dutch colony at one point," she said, slipping into tour-guide mode again. "That's why you see such an influence. The Dutch are very good about celebrating diversity—in people, in culture, and even in food."

Miriam smiled as she scooped some more of the nasi goreng into my bowl and then her own.

The Dutch people were extraordinary, in my opinion. So open-minded. So down to earth. I remembered how Tom had shown such concern for Miriam when he thought I was gawking at her, and later, when the boys who'd loitered outside her window threatened his definition of appropriate behavior in the Red Light District. Was there a code of conduct there?

"Tom seemed to be a big fan of yours," I said. "He's protective of you."

"You mean Tom from the cheese shop across the canal? What makes you think of him?"

"Yes, he tried to kick me out of his store for gawking. I wasn't gawking. I was trying to eat my sandwich somewhere warm, but . . ." I chuckled. "I guess I was actually gawking. I'd just never seen anything like the Red Light District before."

She raised an eyebrow. "Beth, you have prostitution all over your country. You just don't see it. Las Vegas? New Orleans? New York City? San Francisco? Every big city has people walking the streets. Here, we've taken the sex workers off the streets and put them indoors—that is all. It is a far more civilized way to do things if you ask me. Most Dutch people believe it is a human right to do with the body what you want."

I'd never been to any of those places, but what she'd said made sense. Then another thought occurred to me. "I ran into a shop that offered tours of the Red Light District. It seems like a strange thing. What's your take on it?"

"That is what people like Tom are protective about. The tours are controversial."

"How so?"

"Most people in Amsterdam tend to embrace our community. It keeps a lot of violence and danger off the streets. But many people who come to Amsterdam do not understand this." Miriam stood and cleared the bowls and returned with a couple of oranges that she began to peel.

"The tours were founded by a former prostitute as a way of educating people about the history and changes in the sex industry over the years. She wanted to transform the way people thought about the Red Light District. But she was not prepared for how people would respond. Now, instead of using the Red Light District, many come to see it, like Disneyland. It is not an amusement park, and that is why photography is discouraged. It is not respectful."

She passed me an orange. "Have you heard of Mariska Majoor?"

"No, I haven't," I said, peeling off a wedge and popping it in my mouth.

"She is the woman who started the tours. She became a sex worker at sixteen and then later became an advocate for sex workers, founding a union called PROUD. It helps to ensure rights, safety, and equality for workers in the Red Light District. We have access to health care, and we pay taxes. Mariska made a big difference to the way Dutch people viewed the Red Light District." She paused. "Don't get me wrong, not everyone in this country supports the Red Light District, but if they don't, they don't have to come. No one is forcing them."

"A union? I had no idea."

"Most people don't. They think we come here to sell ourselves for money, and they do not consider whether this might not have been a matter of choice. As I told you, I had no choice. My boyfriend forced me into this, and many women are trafficked here by force from all over the world. The government is working to address the trafficking. Not many people use to seek out this profession on their own."

"So what does the union do for you?"

"There are rules that have been developed to protect us. First, there used to be no age limit. Then they made the age limit eighteen, but it was changed to twenty-one in 2013. To work in a window, you have to be registered in a municipality of the Netherlands and have a bank account here. We are not allowed to work more than eleven hours a day even though the windows are open for business from eight in the morning until six in the morning. Also, you have to have a passport so your identity is legitimate. Forced prostitution is illegal. Having a passport helps keep pimps who try to sell women on their own out of here.

"Wow," I said, unable to hide my shock. "It sounds like a real business."

"That is exactly what it is. It is all in the way you look at it. Do you think that men who drive garbage trucks say to themselves, 'I have waited all my life to do this work'? Garbage men make great money in Amsterdam and are able to provide for their families. It is a means to an end. Right? You can spin your story any way you like. Sometimes it makes it easier."

I frowned a little. "What do you mean by that?"

"I am offering comfort to people in need. I am filling a void in some people's lives. It can be as simple as that."

We sat in silence for a moment as I thought about her

story and the pain Miriam had endured. I thought about her parents and siblings. I thought about Mr. Radu, and her boyfriend. How does one recover from that kind of past? How does one trust and offer kindness after that?

I looked her in the eye. "You are really inspiring, Miriam. I mean it."

She looked back at me then stood and retrieved the family photo.

"If you had not heard my story, what would you see?" she asked, handing it to me.

I found it unsettling. The little girls looked different to me now. The parents did too. "Honestly, I would have said that I saw a close, loving family."

"Exactly! Most people who enter this flat see what you saw. When you saw me at the flower market, you saw an accomplished-looking woman. When you saw me in the district, you saw a lesser woman. But I am always the same person." She paused and let her words settle over me before she continued. "You have the power to redirect your path, Beth. All you have to do is change your perspective. I find you inspiring too."

At this, I laughed out loud. There was nothing inspiring about a woman who let her husband lie to her and manipulate her. There was nothing inspiring about giving up. Miriam exemplified everything I wasn't. "How could I inspire anyone?"

"For starters, not having sex for such a long time puts you up there with the nuns, or maybe even at the level of sainthood."

We both laughed at the absurdity of my situation.

"What I'd do for a good roll in the hay," I said, immediately thinking of Luke. The thought caught me off guard. I'd never allowed myself to fantasize about anyone. "I'm not even sure everything works down there."

"Rest assured it's not like a pierced ear."

It took me a few seconds to get the joke, and then I threw back my head and laughed. It felt so good to laugh.

Then my reality came tumbling back. "Should I try to call Troy back now?"

She hesitated. "I'm not sure he's in the right frame of mind to continue the conversation just yet."

I let my head drop and studied the design of her tablecloth. The paisley print seemed to have no pattern—or was I incapable of seeing any order in life after that jarring phone call? No tears fell. No thoughts came. I heard only *You're a pathetic mother and I never want to see you again*. Over and over.

Had Dennis lied to turn Troy against me once and for all? Or had Troy made this up to distract me from whatever had happened to him? All my married life, I'd done what Dennis had asked of me. Why would he want to hurt me?

I had to try to get to the bottom of this.

"Miriam, what should I do?" I asked, feeling sincerely lost.

"If it were me, I would want answers."

"Yes, but my husband doesn't give answers. He knew exactly where Troy was and denied me that information, despite how hard I tried to get it out of him. He denied our son his mother and likely turned him against me. Nothing I ask him will result in the answers I want. He'll deny it all."

"Then don't go back. Forge a new path."

I almost choked on the bite of orange I'd taken. "How? I've spent my whole life following blindly."

"Yes, but tomorrow is another day, so tomorrow you can stop following. Simple as that."

I appreciated how easily she could simplify things in her mind, but in my life, it wouldn't be so easy.

"So, what are you going to do, Beth from California?"

"I don't know. I guess I'll see what happens when I am with Dennis face-to-face."

"Short-term goals are good!" She smiled and stood to grab our coats. "I believe the timing is perfect to catch the last train to Rotterdam."

We walked out into the cold of the evening and headed for the train station. Under normal circumstances, the lit Christmas trees in the windows would have made me smile. Now, the sight just made me sad. Miriam broke the silence.

"I don't know what your plans are, but if you are interested, I am going to a baby shower tomorrow at one o'clock. If you need some company and a diversion, you are welcome to join me."

"I'm not sure I'd be very good company," I said, thinking of the many possible scenarios that awaited me in the hotel room.

"Well, let's say that if you would like to join me, I will meet you at the canal ticket booth at twelve forty-five."

"That is so sweet of you." I reached into my purse,

pulled out a scrap of paper, and scribbled down my address and landline number. "Just in case I don't see you again, this is my address in California. We could write. You could come and visit me."

"Oh dear. Let's not assume that this was our last day together." Miriam took the paper and placed it in her pocket. "Let's assume we will see each other very soon."

She looked down at her watch as the station came into view. "We made record time. The next train doesn't leave for thirty minutes. Come on."

She hooked her arm in mine and headed in a very familiar direction. We crossed the brick bridge over the canal that dropped us into De Wallen.

"Where are you taking me?" I asked, as we neared the windows. I tried not to stare.

"I want to show you the diversity of this place, but we will have to walk briskly. It is Saturday night so the streets are packed. Pretend you are late for an appointment. Quick glances. No staring. OK? What do you see?"

I did as instructed, stealing glances but trying to keep my gaze ahead of me. "Sexy young women, lots of skin."

We turned down a side street and darted through people waiting in a line to get into some sort of show.

"What do you see now?"

The women in the windows here were larger. They moved and posed with attitude and composure. I envied their self-assured manner. What an odd setting to see this kind of self-reliance.

"These are bigger women."

Miriam nodded.

It was easier to steal a peek here, as the street was so full of bystanders. We then walked down a street where there were only women of color, and then a street where the lights in the windows were blue, not red.

"And what do you see here?"

"These women are wearing a lot more makeup. And they all seem to be wearing negligees with flimsy robes. Fancy ones."

"Anything else?" She tilted her chin toward the window of a woman who was framed in a blue light.

"The room is blue, not red. Why is that?"

"Because these are transgender women. Now you can see there is something for everyone. This is a full-service establishment." She looked back at me with a grin. "Now, let's get you back to the station."

As we wove our way through the crowded streets, I was struck by how we could have been anywhere: there were people rushing, people moseying, people window-shopping, people laughing. I could have been at Carmel Village looking for a new jacket. Instead, people were out buying love or comfort. What had Miriam said? It was all about perspective.

When we got to the canal ticket booth, she stopped and pointed to the kiosk. "I will be here tomorrow at 12:45. I hope to see you, Beth from California."

"Thank you for today. I feel like we've been friends forever."

She smiled. "Or perhaps this is a friendship that will last forever."

"Doo eee."
"Doei. *Tot gauw.*"
"What does that mean?"
"See you soon!"

18

Strike Three, You're Out

The hotel looked different as I approached it in darkness. Everything looked different after that phone call with Troy. The Christmas trees in the lobby were in twinkle mode when I walked through. I counted twelve of them but felt no magic. In the elevator, I gazed at my reflection in the mirrors that lined it. I hardly recognized myself—or perhaps I'd never looked at myself from the perspective of someone preparing for a confrontation.

I stood outside our door for a moment and listened. I could hear the hum of the TV. Dennis was in there, probably propped up on the pillows, his ample belly offering a stable surface for a tray. The image filled me with anxiety, so I quickly flashed my key card before I lost my courage.

"Where the hell have you been?" he asked, from the bed. He was wearing only an undershirt and pants that were unbuttoned at the waist. "Do you have any idea what time it is?"

I froze under the anger of his gaze. It latched on to me, a contagion that could soon consume me. I'd spent the train ride back to Rotterdam mentally rehearsing what I had to say, but still I found myself unable to speak. I'd known he'd lead with that very question. He wasn't used to me being anywhere but at his beck and call. He'd never had to wait for me to arrive because I'd always been there for him.

My silence seemed to unglue him, and he sat up, pushing his papers to the side. "I will ask you again: where the hell were you, Beth? It's after eleven."

In my silence, I felt power transfer from him to me. This was a new sensation, and I knew instinctively that I needed to use it to my benefit. All the things I'd planned to say to him dissipated. I'd made up a story about going to the city center in Rotterdam and losing track of time. But then wouldn't I be guilty of lying too?

"I went out."

Looking at him, I slowly pulled off my gloves and set them on the chair near the door before hanging up my coat. I didn't know this person who inhabited my body. Whoever she was, I liked her. When I turned back to the bed, I saw Dennis working at securing the top button of his pants.

"Having trouble?" I asked, in the sweetest of voices. His face grew red. I felt more power transferring my way.

"Shut up, whore! I demand you tell me where you've been."

The ridiculousness of his profane command almost made me burst into laughter, but I kept my composure.

"I have a demand of my own," I said, approaching the bed. "I demand you tell me where Troy is." I looked him straight in the eyes, which looked as if they might pop out of his head.

"What does Troy have to do with this? Beth, seriously, I'm worried about your stability. I think you should go and see someone when we get home."

I felt the power start to shift away and acted quickly to keep it. I went to my purse, removed the form from Sunrise Ranch, and smoothed it out on the desk before handing it to Dennis.

"I demand you tell me why Troy is at Sunrise Ranch," I said, keeping my voice even. "I demand you explain to me why you told our son I didn't want to see him. I demand you tell me why you lied to him about my past."

He blinked in surprise. "Where did you get that?"

For a moment, I thought I had him, but he was quick to recover with a response—too quick. Frighteningly quick. He tossed the paper back to me and I watched it float to the floor.

"Where did you get that?" he asked again.

"Does it matter? Why don't you answer my questions first?"

"I couldn't afford you messing things up. I knew that if you heard he was hurt, you would go to him, and it would draw attention. You'd tell your mother, and she can't keep her mouth shut. Before long, the entire town would know about Troy. It was for your own good."

"My own good?" I consciously kept my voice low, but rage was welling up in me like a wave that had nowhere to travel but out into the world. "You think not seeing my son during his time of need is for my own good?"

"I had my career to consider." He narrowed his eyes. "Can you imagine if anyone caught wind of the fact that Troy caused an accident under the influence? They had proof he was dealing as well. It could ruin everything I've worked for my entire life. I couldn't take the risk." He looked at me as if I were supposed to agree that his life was more important than Troy's. Or mine. I couldn't blame him there. After all, I'd been agreeing with him our whole marriage, not just through my words but also my actions. Or lack thereof.

I shifted gears.

"What about the fact that you told Sunrise Ranch that I had a previous addiction to prescription pills? How can you possibly rationalize the things you said to them?" I thought about looking under Troy's bed and finding the pill containers—and I suddenly remembered that Dennis had been prescribed oxycodone after his carpal tunnel surgery. He'd raved about how the pills made him feel. In front of Troy. He'd renewed the prescription several times. "You're the one who was taking oxycodone. Not me. You brought it into the house, not me."

Again, I thought I had him. Again, he was quick to respond.

"Oxycodone is everywhere. Don't be ignorant, Beth. And anyway, he's a minor, so there were certain stipulations that I had to work around. I had to create a sense of urgency so that Sunrise Ranch would take him. Otherwise, they would have insisted on in-home care." He said this as if it were the most logical thing in the world. As if it were better for Troy to be away from his home, from his family's care.

"You realize that our son thinks I'm an alcoholic and a drug dealer? That his problems stem from my genetic makeup? Did you ever consider how this would affect him? Or me?" I couldn't stop my voice from rising. "These are lies, Dennis! Lies!"

"I had no options. When this all blows over, we'll sort this out once and for all. I did what I had to do to save the family."

I shook my head. "To save the family or to save you? There's a big difference there."

"Well, if it weren't for me, there'd be no family. Isn't that right, Beth? I'm the one who puts food on the table. I'm the one who gives you a good life. I'm the one who gave you a son."

I let his words hang there for a minute. No matter what I said, he'd spin it to suit himself. It appeared I'd gotten my answers, though. Despite the twisted logic, this all fit with the man I now knew Dennis was. I had just one more question.

"Why did you tell me that the old lady wasn't injured?"

He made a shooing gesture. "She was the least of my concerns. She's eighty-five years old and shouldn't have been driving anyways."

"Was she injured badly?"

"Broken arm, three broken ribs, and a fractured hip. I've set her up nicely and have a guarantee that she won't press charges." He smiled a little. "It's all working out as planned, so no need to worry."

That was it. I felt a snap within, as if my heart and soul had disconnected from my body. The fact that the elderly woman's injuries were simply an inconvenience to Dennis left me cold. All the lies and secrets that had filled such a big space were now exposed and disposed of, and there was a void in my heart. I was hollow, without emotion. I had nothing left to say to Dennis. Nothing left to feel toward him.

"I'm going to sleep in the bathtub." I turned away.

"Suit yourself," he said, turning up the TV. "Just don't try any funny stuff, like calling Troy again." I blinked. Sunrise Ranch must have called Dennis to tell him what had happened. Perhaps that is why he was so quick to respond. "You really upset him. I knew you would. Remember, it's your word against mine, and we all know whom people will believe now, don't we? If you want Troy to know the truth at the end of all this, you'll pack your bag and be ready tomorrow because I rebooked our return. We're flying home on the 5:40 p.m. flight."

I heard everything he said but didn't respond. I just walked into the bathroom and quietly locked the door behind me. Then I turned off the light. The night-light by the sink faintly illuminated the space. I slipped off my shoes, lay a clean towel down in the tub, and then used another one to cover myself. For a few moments, I focused on calming my breath. Now, as my tears fell out of me, creating a chill at the nape of my neck, I felt as if I'd come to the conclusion that I was in control of what happened next. It was all up to me.

The tears came without sobs or shudders, without pain. I let them flow, thinking of a quote from *Henry V*: *"Self-love, my liege, is not so vile a sin as self-neglecting."* Funny how these quotes came to revisit me at just the right moment.

It was time for me to change my perspective.

I woke to pounding on the bathroom door. I pulled myself out of the porcelain tub and let Dennis in so he could use the bathroom. As he busied himself, I sat on the side of the bed and stared at the train station.

Thoughts drifted through my head.

I'm leaving the Netherlands today.

I can return to my life as Dennis's wife. I can return to a mother who urged me to live on a man's terms. I can return to a life without Troy, and I can live with that until Dennis chooses to change that.

Or I can change everything myself.

I was sure Dennis's rebooking of the tickets had everything to do with what was good for him. If I was going to live a life that was good for me, it was up to me to make that happen.

Dennis came out of the bathroom groomed for the day. His suitcase was packed, and all the hangers in the closet dangled empty, like the insides of my soul.

"I have to go to the corporate office for a final briefing to set the calendar for the next year. The CEO agreed to meet before he goes to church and then I'll be back. You need to be packed and ready to go by two o'clock. The car will take us to the airport."

I didn't answer. Kept staring out the window. I could tell by the flags below that there was a light breeze, and the sun was battling for inclusion this morning. I wished it were raining. I wished the wind were blowing so hard that I had to hold on to something to stay upright. I wished that it were blowing so hard that it would blow me away from here.

I was done with my husband. I didn't know exactly what that meant yet.

"So I can count on you to be ready by two o'clock, Beth? Can you handle that?" Out of the corner of my eye, I saw him straighten his tie in the mirror and brush his shoulders free of any lingering flakes of skin.

"Beth!"

I'd never realized how agitated silence made him. I'd never tested those waters before. I nodded but didn't look at him. I couldn't bear to look into those lying eyes.

"OK, we'll be back in California before you know it." There he was, talking as if nothing had been uncovered last night, as if he hadn't offered me up as a sacrificial lamb in exchange for his career, his reputation.

As soon as I heard the door shut, I ordered room service. I'd never done this before either, but today was the first day as a new me. My night in the bathtub had produced a resolve. I felt like one of the pebbles that Troy had put in the rock tumbler I'd bought him for his seventh birthday. For weeks, the rough pebbles tossed in the frothy solution, knocked against the sides of the mixer, day after day, until the time finally came to dump them into the sink and rinse them to expose their smooth, polished surfaces. I took a long, hot shower and willed my transformation to begin.

After I got dressed and packed, I sat down and wrote a letter on the hotel stationery and then looked at my hand, rolling my wedding ring back and forth. I slipped it off my finger and considered putting it into the envelope with the letter. Then I dropped it in my toiletry bag, which I zipped up and placed in my suitcase.

I set the envelope on top of one of Dennis's bags and scanned the room. On the nightstand was the Rolex watch I'd given him for his fiftieth birthday. I contemplated taking it with me to pawn, but that wouldn't feel right. I wanted to start this new life with this new Beth on my terms. I wasn't vindictive. I'd given him that watch in another life, when I was unaware that mine was being robbed.

With my bag zipped up, my coat and hat on, and my gloves in my pocket, I headed for the elevator. In the lobby, a voice called out "Mrs. Strum." I froze in my tracks. The guy who'd given me the phone number was standing at the desk, waving.

"Can I help you, Mrs. Strum?"

"Oh no, I'm fine."

I watched him look at his books and then back up at me.

"We have a car coming around two o'clock for you. You're a bit early. Can I take your suitcase and store it behind the desk? Mr. Strum asked me to keep an eye on you," he said with a wink, as if I were getting the VIP treatment, but I knew Dennis's motive. All the pieces were plain as day now, so easy to interpret.

"No, thank you. I'm actually meeting Mr. Strum later." I turned to walk away, but the guy was relentless.

"Mrs. Strum . . ."

I could either lie or just keep walking. And since I wasn't good at lying, I walked fast through the glass doors and into the cool morning air. Before heading to the station, I made a quick stop at an ATM to withdraw the maximum amount that the machine allowed. My heels clicked on the pavement in staccato, reminding me of Miriam on the first day I met her. I had equated the sound with confidence and resolve. Could it be that I, too, had some resolve blossoming inside me?

I arrived in Amsterdam at eleven o'clock and secured my suitcase in a locker at the station before emerging into daylight. I smiled as I looked out at the city that had won my heart. I had no idea how this day was going to end. All I knew was that I was going to trust myself. If I did, everything would work out. First things first—I needed to visit the flower market. I didn't want to show up to a baby shower empty-handed. If panic set in or my gut told me to go, I'd head back to Rotterdam and meet Dennis by two o'clock.

The flower market was a burst of colors on this brisk yet sunny day, and I had the man who worked there create a bouquet of flowers that I chose by name: tulips, roses, snowdrops, peonies, and grape hyacinths. He enhanced the bouquet with ivy and sprigs of baby's breath. I walked slowly to the meeting point, stopping on bridges to take in the scenery and soak up the energy. Amsterdam had opened a whole new world in which to explore and find myself. Amsterdam spoke to me from every church steeple and every bike that wheeled by: *Welcome, Beth. Make yourself at home.*

19

A Birth

As I approached the kiosk I saw her, stunning as ever. She was such a beautiful woman, and she embraced life in a way that I hadn't known was possible. She was the reason I didn't feel sorry for myself right now. I was flying by the seat of my pants, and perhaps I'd regret my actions, but they were going to be mine to regret.

She was scanning the entrance of the station when I approached her from behind.

"Hello, Miriam!"

"Hoi"—she whirled around, and her eyes brightened—"Beth! I'm so glad you came. And what beautiful flowers. You already have been to the flower market?"

I nodded. "I got here early, so I decided to get some flowers for the hostess. We're still on for the baby shower, right?"

"Yes, of course. Let's walk. I hate being late, so I'll fill you in on our way. It's not too far."

We walked away from the station, in the general direction of Miriam's flat. Then we crossed one of the canal bridges and headed north along a green space with tree-lined paths. It felt so nice to be walking by her side and pretending that everything was as it should be.

"The hostess of the baby shower is one of my dearest friends," Miriam explained. "She's from Thailand, and she shared a window with me when I first started. Her older sister had been brought here to work in the Red Light District, but my friend was never able to reconnect with her. Sometimes the world just swallows people up."

I nodded sadly. "Isn't that the truth."

"Her name is Malee," Miriam continued, "which means *flower* in Thai, but we all call her May. She has done very well for herself. Unlike me, she stays in touch with her family and even visits on occasion. They think she is an office clerk. It is easier that way. No harm in letting them think what they want." She smiled at me and shrugged. "We all do what we have to do. I believe you Americans say, 'Follow your own drummer?'"

"Yes," I said, "or, 'Follow the beat of your own drum.' Does she still search for her sister?"

Miriam shook her head. "She has let go of that dream but offers the universe her desire to be reunited with her one day. She is very spiritual. I know you will love her. You will notice a tattoo on her neck—the initials *RS*. Her pimp marked her before she came to the Netherlands, to keep track of her. She tells everyone that the letters stand for 'really sweet.'"

I grabbed my neck and rubbed it, imagining the pain of needles marking me forever. "I cannot imagine someone forcing me to tattoo their initials on my body."

"It's not so common anymore, now that the Dutch government has cracked down on pimps bringing foreign women into the district. Things are a lot better now."

It was awful to think of women being branded, like cattle to be sold. How could anyone believe that they owned another person?

"The woman who is pregnant is also a sex worker, and she is Dutch."

"Really?"

Was her pregnancy an accident? I mean, I didn't even really think about it until now, but in your profession, precaution must be a big prerequisite?"

"Oh yes, that is true. But Anke chose to have a baby. She has been a sex worker for nine years, and she also chose this. Five years ago, a client fell in love with her. For four years he courted her and then, when he became a widower, he asked her to be his wife. She said no but told him that she would have his baby. He is older and wealthy. She will be well taken care of."

Once again, my mind was blown. "I assume she's no longer a sex worker?"

"Well, of course, now she is very pregnant, but she is considering a return to the profession. She is not sure what she wants to do yet. Speaking of plans, what are yours, Beth from California?" she said, looking at me. "How did it go last night? You are here, so I assume it went well."

I exhaled. "It depends on how you look at it. I got my questions answered, but my plan is still up in the air. But let's talk about that later." I was feeling that to get clarity, I needed space from thinking about it. "What did you get for Anke?" I nudged my chin toward the wrapped box in her hands. Then I glanced at my watch and saw that it was almost one o'clock. If I was flying home tonight with Dennis, I'd have to leave in thirty minutes to get back to Rotterdam in time to meet the car.

Or I could stay longer and take the train directly to the airport and meet him at the gate, I thought, giving myself a bit more leeway.

"Oh, I have made the baby a rosary with beads the color of her mother's and father's eyes."

Another surprise. "I didn't know you were religious."

"I am not so much, but Anke is. I found this wonderful bead shop that had a great variety of blue and green beads. When the baby uses her rosary, she will have her mother and father watching over her. Most of us prefer to give handmade gifts. The father will probably take care of all the other stuff."

I was touched by the idea and excited to see what other handmade items would be gifted to the baby today. Thinking about the possibilities, I realized that I didn't have a talent I could put to use if I were asked to make a handmade gift. That was something else I wanted to change.

I thought about my own baby shower. All the guests

had bought me huge plastic, over stimulating gifts that sat around and collected dust. As he got older, Troy preferred his BRIO trains and DUPLOs. Diana, the wife of West Tech Systems' CFO, had hosted the shower and offered a steady stream of mimosas that soon turned into glasses of champagne. It seemed the guests had come to party rather than celebrate my baby and me. Most were buzzed before we started opening gifts. One person even threw up in the bathroom. I'd been waiting outside the bathroom to pee, which I had to do frequently in those days, and when the occupant opened the door, she had to hold the door jamb to stay upright. Meanwhile, her face was a waxy shade of gray. When I closed the door to relieve myself, the distinct smell of vomit had me peeing in record time so I could get out of there.

Diana had hired an event planner to do the whole thing, and a sure sign of the disconnect was the cake, on which my name had been spelled wrong. How do you misspell Beth? Who's named Bett, anyway? Everyone laughed at the error. Someone commented that Bett was better than Butt. It was of no concern to them. I tried to focus on the effort that had been made.

I'd still hoped to connect with these women somehow, but as I opened my gifts, most of them migrated to the other room to refill their glasses and gossip, never to return to share the moment with me. As I unwrapped the last gift, only three women were left in the room, and one was on her phone. Then Diana stuck her head in the living room and asked, "Are you done opening presents yet?" When I said yes, she announced, "OK, let's get this party started! Bring your glasses in the kitchen and get some more champagne." She obviously hadn't been talking to me. I'd been so relieved when the shower was over. But I never said a negative word about it to Dennis because he would have accused me of being ungrateful.

"Well, here we are," Miriam said, bringing me back to the moment. "Are you ready to meet some of my friends?" She gestured in the direction of a set of steps that led to a tall, narrow facade of brick that held a wooden door with a wreath on it. The wreath was made with real branches and berries.

"Ready."

Miriam rang the bell and May answered with a smile.

"This is my friend Beth," Miriam announced, after giving May a hug. "She's so happy to join us today."

May beamed. "And I am so happy that you will help us celebrate this wonderful occasion."

Her voice was soft and velvety, like a smooth ganache that you let rest on your tongue. I immediately spotted the tattoo; it was hard to miss, not pretty or artistically done. I quickly shifted my gaze and our eyes met. They were full of kindness and light. They made me smile.

May took my coat and ushered us into the living room, where several women were gathered. I instantly spotted Anke, her belly a dead giveaway. She was dressed in a grayish blue maternity dress with a light knitted vest that hung to the hem. Her eyes twinkled as she mingled with her friends. The room was filled with a feeling of love, and I just wanted to sit down and soak up all the good vibes floating from woman to woman.

A mound of presents sat on a round table in front of a bay window that offered a view of the road from which we'd come. There was a Christmas tree decorated with red ribbons and what looked like cookies and pinecones. There was also a small fireplace with a cozy fire crackling in it and a mantel adorned with twinkling lights threaded through pine branches. Once again, I wasn't sure what I'd expected a prostitute's home to look like, but I certainly hadn't expected this.

My eyes lit with surprise as I caught sight of a familiar face. A few feet away stood the owner of Les Petites Chattes, speaking with another woman. I recognized her even though I could only see her profile. Our conversation came back to me, and I remembered that she'd seemed to be an advocate for the sex-worker community. *She must have made friends with the sex workers when they patronized her store*, I thought.

"What do you see?" Miriam asked me.

"Oh," I said, a bit embarrassed to have been caught staring. "I recognize that lady. I went into her shop in search of something and she was so kind."

"Oh, Maria. Yes, she used to work in the windows but was able to achieve her dream of being a shop owner. Most of her jewelry and crafts are made by women from the windows. We are a very resourceful bunch."

There was that smirk! I finally understood the secret. Polite discretion. These women were valued despite their occupation—or maybe because of it. They also weren't defined by their work. They had so much to offer. I wanted to wrap myself in this moment, to just keep watching these women, who'd come together in such a loving way. My baby shower hadn't contained an ounce of sincerity, unless you counted the women's sincere interest in keeping their champagne glasses full.

"May I offer you some spiced apple cider?" May asked, coming up by my side. "It's a specialty here during the holiday." She smiled and added, "You can have it warm or cold."

"Warm, please."

"And you, Miriam?"

"Warm too, May. Thank you."

May returned with our drinks minutes later. I'd expected the "spiced" apple cider to be steeped in liquor, but to my surprise it was liquor free. Another inaccurate assumption. Scanning the room, I noticed most of the women held mugs and were very much engaged in their conversations. I'd been envisioning the stereotype of prostitutes I'd been exposed to over the years on TV or in movies—women who were hard, tough, uncaring, opportunistic, seedy. I'd assumed that most struggled with substance abuse. Yet another example of my ignorant typecasting. I'd thought Miriam might be an exception to the rule, but all these women seemed lovely. They could have held their own at any corporate dinner. They were poised, well dressed, and invested in each other. Instantly, I felt guilty for my assumptions. The women at *my* baby shower, all wives of upper management and directors, didn't hold a candle to these women when it came to kindness and class.

Soon, we were asked to sit, and the hum of conversation settled. May then welcomed everyone and introduced the lady of the hour. She also introduced me, explaining that I was an out-of-town friend of Miriam's, and many women nodded and sent smiles in my direction. Then May passed around trays bearing a variety of finger food and we played games. For the first one, each of us had to cut a piece of string to the length we thought was required to encircle Anke's belly. The winner of each game received a small wrapped gift—a ceramic candleholder big enough to hold a votive and decorated with a pattern similar to that of my reindeer. Laughter swirled around the room. I looked at my watch. It was one thirty. Taking the train back to Rotterdam was no longer an option. I would have to meet Dennis at the airport.

We played another game and May circulated with her trays of delicacies again. She'd added petit fours to one of the trays—some kind of pink-white-and-light-green squares that were absolutely delicious. An attentive hostess, she'd close her eyes briefly and bow ever so slightly each time someone took something from her tray.

Glancing at the window, I noticed the sky had changed. It looked as if it was going to snow. That's when I noticed the pair of reindeer on the table in front of the bay window, pushed off to the side, likely to make way for the packages. It stunned me to see them there—exactly the pair that usually occupied my kitchen window. An odd sensation came over me. Then I remembered that the shop owner had said that a woman in the community made these during the holidays. Was May the artist?

It was time for presents. Anke opened each one carefully while chatting about all sorts of wonderings she had about becoming a mother. It was as if she were talking to her sisters, and I was one of them. I looked at my watch. It was two o'clock. Plenty of time. Now that I wasn't going to Rotterdam first, the train ride would be only twenty-one minutes to the airport.

The room responded to a knitted yellow-and-green sweater and cap with a collective "Ahh." The set was passed around the room, and many of the ladies caressed the soft items and held them up to their cheeks, including me. Someone had embroidered a needlepoint scene for the nursery; it looked as if it could have hung in a museum. There were handmade blankets and curtains, a carved rattle, Miriam's rosary, and a thin handmade box that held a CD containing lullabies. Anke asked May if she could sample it, and May quickly put it in the CD player on the other side of the room. The music was Dutch folk renditions of nursery rhymes and lullabies, including "Mary Had a Little Lamb" and "Hush Little Baby."

When "Rock-A-Bye Baby" came on, Anke stood, moved to the center of the circle of chairs in the room, and began to sway, explaining that the song reminded her of her mother, who had passed away recently after a lengthy battle with cancer. She let her head drop back and closed her eyes while she rocked to the music. I could see small wet streams make their way down her cheeks, but she kept smiling. One by one, the other ladies stood and began to rock. They joined hands and encircled Anke and then slowly closed around her in a group hug. I found myself rising to join the circle. It was a summoning of souls. We were all witnesses to Anke's tender reverie. I was overcome with love and peace. It was the most beautiful moment I'd experienced among friends.

When the song ended, Anke sat back down and the rest of us joined her so she could unwrap her last package, which was from May. She'd sewn a teddy bear. It had soft beige fur and a red bow. The smile on the bear's face brought tears to my eyes. It looked just like a bear that I'd bought for Troy when he turned one. I took a deep breath and settled myself.

"We shall call it May," Anke announced, as she held it up. Then she hugged it.

Finally, May brought out a beautiful almond torte, and after dessert, Anke began to say goodbye to her guests who had commitments.

Miriam had officially introduced me to Maria earlier, as well as some of the other ladies. As people began to leave, Maria made her way over to me.

"Did you ever find a replacement for your reindeer?" she asked. "The artist is the one stepping out the door." She pointed to a tall woman with red hair and willowy limbs.

"No, unfortunately," I said. "But I did purchase a replica of the Oude Kerk. That will have to be my souvenir."

"When do you return to America? Or will you be here for the Christmas holiday?"

"That's a good question." I glanced at my watch and saw that it was three o'clock. I was cutting it close. "I'm not sure."

She accepted my answer, and after she bade me farewell, I walked over to the window to get a closer look at the reindeer. May was gathering small plates and pieces of wrapping paper from the floor.

"I love your reindeer pair," I said to her.

"Yes, they were a gift from a client of mine."

"Oh, I have a pair too."

She smiled. "Did you just get them on your visit here? The artist only sells them during the holidays."

"No, my husband gave them to me as a souvenir after one of his business trips. I recently broke one and tried to find a replacement during my stay here, but when I finally found the shop, there were no reindeer left."

"Why don't you take mine? Which one broke?"

"The standing one but no, I could never take that from you. And anyway, the need to find a replacement will give me a reason to come back."

"Are you sure? I would love for you to have it. Really." She bowed again and closed her eyes briefly, holding out the reindeer.

"I'm positive! Thank you, though. You are so generous."

"Perhaps your husband will bring you one next year?" May offered. "Does he visit Amsterdam often during the holidays?"

"Actually, he does. But he also passes through Amsterdam en route to other destinations throughout the year." It was weird to be speaking so calmly about my husband, as if nothing had happened that had changed the course of my life. Maybe nothing had? What was I doing here? Out of the corner of my eye, I saw Miriam shoot May a glance, and their eyes connected.

Feeling uneasy, I looked at my watch again. I'd still be able to catch the train and head straight to the gate at the airport.

I needed to go.

I went to get my coat, and when I came back into the room, Miriam and May were talking quietly, foreheads almost touching. Their expressions were serious, concerned, not in line with the mood of the lovely gathering of friends.

What was going on? What was the reason for secrets now?

Miriam and I said our goodbyes and thank-yous and headed out into the cool air. I was going to have to walk quickly if I was going to catch the next train to the airport.

"Did you have fun?" Miriam asked, breaking the silence that had fallen between us.

"Yes." I smiled distractedly. "It was like nothing I've ever experienced."

"I am so glad. And where to now? We have yet to discuss your plans. Are you heading back to Rotterdam?"

It was nagging at me, the way May and Miriam had been looking at each other and whispering. We'd just crossed a bridge when I stopped in my tracks.

"Miriam? What were you and May whispering about?"

Miriam looked at me quickly. So quickly that it stunned me into my next question.

"What are you not telling me?"

Miriam's face got red, and I saw her eyes well up with tears. "Nothing, Beth. Let's just drop it, OK?"

But this new version of me couldn't drop it. "Miriam,

please tell me what's going on." As the words came out of my mouth it hit me: their interaction had occurred during the discussion about the porcelain reindeer. "Wait, do you know the client who gave May those reindeer?"

It was brief, but I saw panic in her eyes for a moment. The secret had to do with me, and it was paining her to be honest.

"Beth, let's talk about you. What happened last night?"

"No, Miriam," I said curtly. "I don't want to talk about last night. I want to talk about what just happened."

"Nothing happened, Beth. Let it rest. You have a lot on your mind." She seemed to be struggling to keep her composure.

And in that moment, I knew.

"You know who gave her those reindeer, don't you?" I didn't wait for her answer but opened my purse and retrieved my wallet. I pulled out a plastic protector containing a picture of Dennis, Troy, and me taken several years ago for our Christmas card. While Troy had changed, Dennis and I looked about the same. "Is this the client?" I pointed to Dennis.

She looked at the picture then looked away. "Beth, do not do this. Not now."

"Do what?" I heard my voice, and it was barely recognizable. Hard and cold and mean. "Ask for the truth? Don't you think I deserve the truth? After all these lies, don't you think I'm worthy of the truth?"

When she turned to face me, tears were streaming down her face. "You have been hurt so much. It is not fair to add more hurt to your heart." She wiped her face, but the tears kept coming.

"Is her client . . . Dennis?" I whispered. I already knew the answer. It all made sense now.

"Do not blame May, Beth."

"I don't," I said, and meant it. "She was doing her job, right? How long?" I also knew the answer to this. It would explain why I hadn't had sex for all these years.

"Awhile. I am sorry, Beth. I had no idea, nor did May. How could we? What can I do?"

A feeling was building inside of me—a bright, fiery stream of lava that had hit water and was turning hard, black, dark, and ugly. I couldn't stop it.

"I need to go to the train station." I turned and walked away.

"Can I walk with you?" she called out anxiously. "Please?"

I didn't turn around. I just walked.

20

A New Backbone

One single piece of information had altered me forever. I'd been coming undone for years, but it had pulled away the final thread. Any hope I might have had regarding my marriage, any thoughts of trying to fix things, had dissipated like fog when I found out that Dennis had been visiting the Red Light District for years.

I'd based my entire reality on what others had said was important instead of figuring that out for myself. Now, at thirty-eight, I'd grown a backbone in record time. A desire to control my destiny. I'd just had a growth spurt, of sorts.

I sat in the train station for a while, my suitcase at my side, watching the time tick away on my watch, as if paying homage to a life that I was choosing to part ways with. My two selves had been having quite a discussion. Should Do was safe and powerless. Could Do was risky but in my control. Should Do might or might not offer a reunion with Troy. Could Do would find a way to make that happen.

Over the last few days, I'd heard stories of struggles that had been worse than mine, and when I considered the people these women had become, I understood that the choice was clear. Of course, my need to reunite with Troy and make sure he had what he needed to heal was not a small issue, but I had faith that I could figure it out. I had to start with me.

When the clock in the station sounded, I looked up. It was 5:30 p.m. It seemed as if a rush of people had taken flight, just like the plane to the States that was scheduled to lift off shortly. I let myself imagine free-falling from the plane, the cold air removing all my murky thoughts as I sped toward earth, and then landing on my feet in the train station right in front of myself. The Beth who stood before me was strong, willing to face the challenges before her. I closed my eyes in an effort to merge the two selves. When I opened my eyes, the station was void of my alter ego.

Perhaps, she'd joined me or perhaps she'd left, but what was important was that she was no longer a separate entity to be seen.

The sound of the suitcase wheels rolling over the cobblestones kept me focused. I summoned all my courage as I neared Miriam's house. Soft yellow light glowed through the living room window. She hadn't plugged in her tree. I was just relieved she was home.

I stood outside Miriam's window and looked inside. She was in her chair, her back to me. Her shadow moved across the room as she got up. She disappeared for a moment then returned with a warm cloth to place on her eyes. Just yesterday, she'd done that for me. I waited until my body could no longer stay still in the cold. I either had to go in or get moving. I'd considered going to the hotel and getting a room, but I felt a need to talk to Miriam first, after having left her so abruptly. She'd been caught in the middle of something that wasn't her fault, and I owed her the decency of an explanation.

I climbed the three steps and knocked. When she opened the door, she collapsed into my arms, sobbing.

"I am so sorry, Beth. You do not deserve this."

I rubbed her back as she had rubbed mine and waited for her to calm down. Then she ushered me in and closed the door and we settled in the living room. I'd left my suitcase outside on the covered stoop, well out of sight.

I met her gaze. Her face was swollen, as if she had a bad case of poison oak around her eyes. "I hope it's OK I came by unannounced," I said. "I was sitting at the train station awhile."

She nodded. "I thought I would never see you again. I thought you would fly back to America and forever hate me."

"I am full of hate, but not for you." I looked at my watch. It was 6:45 p.m. If the plane had left on time, it was on its way back to California. Right now, I had no desire to think about Dennis and how he'd reacted to the note I'd left. I had no desire to think about whether he cared that I wasn't on the flight. The hate was still too raw and unbridled. I didn't trust it.

"Finding out about May and my husband was the final straw," I said, looking at Miriam again. "But if it hadn't been that, another lie would have eventually broken us. Knowing what I know now, I just couldn't bear to go back." I glanced at the dark tree. "Can we plug that in? I need some light in my life."

Miriam jumped up and brought the tree to life. Suddenly, the room was cozier, and I sighed with relief.

"Would you like some tea? I have a special mix of chamomile with a hint of peppermint. Sound good?"

I nodded, and she went off to the kitchen to heat the water. I exhaled. There was something very safe about this place. I knew that Miriam wouldn't hurt me in any way, and I needed that security right now, to help me build my strength. She returned with a mug, and I could tell she'd added some honey from the smell that wafted up to greet me. I felt my muscles relax further.

We sat in silence for a few minutes until I could no longer hold my thoughts in.

"What I don't understand is why," I said, inhaling the steam and then sighing. "Why would Dennis go and sleep with strangers when he had me, a willing partner, the person he chose to marry?"

This was the question that had been looping in my mind ever since I found out. Was May that much more attractive than I was?

Miriam was staring at me. She shook her head and bit her lip before she spoke.

"Who knows the reasoning behind why your husband

came to the district. Some men claim that sex with their wife becomes routine—that it is like telling a story you already know. When they come to us, they are looking for something different. Not knowing the story is exciting, I suppose."

"Well, that doesn't apply to Dennis because we really only had sex once, and that was the night Troy was conceived. After that there were a couple of feeble attempts, but nothing came of them and that was that."

She lifted a shoulder. "For some, it is about fulfilling a fantasy. They have their choice of whatever type of woman they want. You saw the diversity in the windows. It is like a child in a candy store—so much to choose from. They do not have to worry about rejection as long as they have money to pay for it."

I exhaled. "Well, Dennis has plenty of that and he loves to flaunt it whenever he can." It made a lot of sense to me that Dennis would be turned on by the control, especially when he could manipulate it with money.

Miriam continued. "And some men find it easier to have sex with a woman in the window than with their wives," she said gently. "With us, they have nothing to lose. With their wives, there are lots of expectations. Think about a dog that has the choice to jump through a series of hoops to get a treat or to get a treat from the trainer straightaway. What do you think the dog will choose?"

I considered her analogy. "When you put it that way, it seems like an easy choice, but think about the wife at home who knows nothing about this choice—the wife who would do anything to have her husband desire her. That was me, Miriam. I was that wife." I wiped away a lone tear.

Miriam nodded thoughtfully, and we sat in silence for a bit. Finally, she said, "Some men do not come for sex, Beth. I had a man who just asked me to stroke his head while I played Jim Croce music softly. Another man once paid me to listen to him sing with his shirt off. Everyone has their own story. I have learned to hold back on passing judgment on people until their actions have earned it. I once had a man who wanted me to talk like a baby to him—that was my limit. We all have those too."

"It's just so hard to believe that for all those years, I kept saving myself for my husband while he was giving himself to someone else. What's wrong with me?" I felt my eyes fill and willed my hatred to come back. Anger felt safe.

"Beth, men would pay big money to be with someone as beautiful as you. There is no doubt in my mind. So remove the thought from your head that anything is wrong with you."

"You're just being nice." I imagined myself in a window and saw only an awkward woman with no confidence.

"So, how does it work anyway?" I asked, intrigued again. "How do you go about setting the expectations with clients? Do they make an offer and you counter?" Then I laughed without humor. "I can't imagine Dennis bartering for anything."

"The transactions are controlled and clear. There is a baseline rate of fifty euros for fifteen or twenty minutes. A condom must be in place and clothes on. Everything else costs money. Want to touch a breast? It will cost you money. You want clothes off? More money. More time will cost you more money. Lots of sex workers do not like to kiss. They take that off the table right away. Some women do not like working the night shift out of fear of the drunken tourists who mostly frequent the district after dark. Everything is a negotiation."

I thought of the juice place near my house, where patrons could buy the regular smoothie and then add protein, chia seeds, sprouts, etc.—all at a price. The business model was universal!

"I guess you have good business sense." I smiled weakly.

"Do not be under the impression that this is an easy life, Beth. There are almost three hundred windows in the Red Light District, and there is a woman in each of those windows. Sometimes two, as some windows are shared. There is lots of competition. It costs about one hundred euros to rent a window during the day, on a side street in the district. More if you get closer to the busy center of the district and more at night. You do the math. It is not an easy life," she repeated. "A sex worker might need four to five clients a day just to pay the rent."

"I didn't mean that," I said quickly, flushing. "I just know nothing about it."

"I know you are curious. I just do not want you to get the wrong impression. My life is very different now than it was when I started."

"The perfect revenge," I said, mostly to myself.

Miriam looked at me and frowned. "I think I know what

you are talking about. But revenge is a dangerous thing."

I met her gaze and laughed. "I was just imagining Dennis strolling by and seeing me in a window. Being able to reject him would be my revenge."

Miriam narrowed an eye. I could tell she was struggling with a response. Not that I could blame her. The suggestion was absurd.

"Not to change the subject," she said, "but what *are* your plans for the evening?" She glanced up at her antique clock and I followed her gaze. It was almost ten.

I finally told her everything that had transpired with Dennis the night before and explained that I wasn't sure what I'd do next. She regarded me quietly and then excused herself.

My heart sunk. I'd made a huge mistake. All my questions, not to mention my state of mind, had made Miriam uncomfortable. She was probably in the other room calling her friends and asking them to come and remove me. Was it too late to get a room at the hotel? I stood to return my mug to the kitchen and make my exit, but just then Miriam appeared in the hall and beckoned me to follow. I walked to the doorway of the extra bedroom and noticed that she'd made up the day bed and cleared the desk. She'd also lit a small candle on the nightstand.

"Your room awaits you. We will figure out getting you the things that you may need tomorrow."

I breathed another sigh of relief and gave her a hug.

Pulling away, I said, "That won't be necessary." I walked to the front door, opened it, and retrieved my suitcase.

"Well, Beth from California, you are more resourceful and equipped than you know!" She hugged me again and helped me settle in, insisting that I empty my suitcase and hang my things in the closet. "Tomorrow, we will talk about your next step, but tonight, you will rest and dream good thoughts."

I wanted to believe her, but as soon as I turned out the light and blew out the candle, all I could think of was Dennis in the Red Light District. It set my heart racing. What hurt the most was the fact that I'd believed in us the whole seventeen years of our marriage. I'd thought that what we had was love. He hadn't left like my father had, so things had to be good enough. At least that's what my mother had insisted, whenever I questioned my marriage.

Staying together didn't equal love. I realized that now. My life was a mere illusion, a shadow of a life, one void of partnership and intimacy. It had felt so solid, so permanent, but then it had changed so quickly, so easily, like a channel changed with a remote.

I wanted to ask May what it was that she'd done for him, but I knew I couldn't. That wouldn't be fair to her. Plus, I wasn't sure I could ever speak to her again—not because of her, but because I'd see Dennis in everything she said and did, and this was an image I needed to rid myself of. Immediately.

I wanted a fresh start. I wanted a chance to make it on my own. To make that happen, I'd need to return home at some point, but for now, I was here, and that was where I intended to stay for the time being.

Here, with a prostitute. Of all the people in the world, this person, who was beautiful inside and out, had been instrumental in helping to save me. Most people in my old life wouldn't believe it if I told them. I was still wrapping my head around it. One thing I knew—Miriam didn't hold back kindness and empathy, something I'd been hard-pressed to find in my old world.

I woke twice in the night, after bad dreams. I couldn't remember the dreams exactly, but there was a sense of darkness. And Dennis. I must have called out because after the second nightmare, Miriam crawled into bed with me. When I woke again, it was light out and Miriam was gone. She'd left a note saying that she had some commitments and would be back later in the afternoon.

A few days passed. I tried to get out of the flat for a walk each day, but really, I just wanted to hide under the covers and melt away. One morning, in an attempt to distract myself, I stopped at a craft shop and bought an intricate paint-by-number picture of a vase of tulips. I found I was actually pretty good at painting in those tiny areas. It made me wonder what else I might be good at. Perhaps I'd buy some fabric and try my hand at sewing. This type of self assessment was overdue!

In the evenings, Miriam and I would make dinner together then sit and talk. It would never take long before the conversation shifted to Dennis and Troy. Miriam attempted to relieve me of the sadness in my weary little life, listening with a patient ear.

One evening we went caroling along the canals with

some of her friends. Most of the carols were in Dutch, but we did sing "Joy to the World" in English, and I sang more loudly than anyone. Another evening we went ice skating, but memories of Troy as a child and thoughts of the current state of our relationship soured my mood.

Meanwhile, my anxiety grew. I'd never been away for the holiday. What was Dennis doing? Did he miss me? What had he told everyone? And where was Troy? Did he wish he were home celebrating with us? Collecting the bounty of Dennis's overindulgence? While I missed Troy so much it hurt, I knew that there wasn't much else tying me to my home anymore. The house was like a big box of lies wrapped up beautifully and placed under the tree for the sake of appearances. And so, I resolved to make the most of Christmas in Amsterdam.

After dinner on Christmas Eve, Miriam brought out a clay bottle of Dutch gin and two small tumblers. We'd eaten a delicious meal of ground beef and vegetables wrapped in cabbage leaves and pickled beets, which Miriam had picked up from a nearby eatery. As we sipped the gin in the cozy living room, I felt the slow burn of the alcohol loosen my angst. I sat back and welcomed the evening.

"What will the Red Light District be like tonight?" I asked, turning to Miriam. "Busy? Dead?"

She chuckled. "That is the beauty of our community. It changes from day to day. You may have clients that you see every Wednesday at three o'clock and you may have a one-and-done encounter. Tonight could be busy or dead, depending on what the world needs. Working in this business forces you to live in the present. Do you want to take a stroll and see?"

"Oh no, I just wondered if—never mind. I have no business asking these questions."

"Of course you do. I have nothing to hide." Miriam looked at me and beamed, neutralizing my hesitation.

"OK," I said with a grin. "So then may I ask whether you have a favorite client? Someone you see regularly?"

"That is an easy one. Robert."

"Tell me about Robert—unless you want to hear more about my sad life?"

We both chuckled.

"Robert and I met quite a while ago. I had only been working in the window for a couple of years when he showed up disheveled and broken, like a sad hippie, and I almost did not open the door for fear that he smelled. That is something I cannot tolerate. But there was something in his eyes that told me he needed a friend. Kind of like how you looked when I met you at the coffee shop. Same look."

"What's his story?" I asked, taking another sip of my gin.

"He was a psychiatric doctor who worked on the other side of town. He had a flourishing practice and a beautiful family. Then one day, his life as he knew it was ripped away from him. That morning, a bus drifted into oncoming traffic and hit a car at full speed, killing the three occupants." She dropped her head slightly. "His wife, his four-year-old son, and their three-month-old baby girl. She was taking their son to preschool when it happened."

My heart twisted, and I swallowed more gin. "That's terrible. How does someone ever recover from something like that?"

"It is a process. For Robert, he shifted his focus in his practice, so he now has a business in grief counseling. It seems to be cathartic for him. It is what he needs to do to move on. Healing does not happen overnight. He has had some dark days to endure."

"If you don't mind my asking, what makes him your favorite?" I asked, feeling the gin creep deeper into my head.

"It is hard to put into words." She paused. "We have both survived trauma, and we bonded because of this. Our time together is a mutual exchange. He gives me something and I give him something. He is the kindest man I know, and beyond that, he is a very attentive lover. He loves seeing my pleasure. That is not something that I come across often in my profession."

I took another sip. Pleasure wasn't something I could imagine either. Did I even feel deserving of it? For so long, I had accepted my lot in life, as my mother had taught me to.

"Did he remarry?" I asked.

"No, that is the farthest thing from his mind."

"Would you consider marrying him if he asked you, though?" The fuzz in my head was growing.

She shook her head. "Oh no. Marriage is not something that I desire. Independence has always been my focus."

"I wonder what that would be like, to have intimacy on that level," I said, again almost to myself. "I can't imagine . . . I have no idea how to feel comfortable with another human in that way. If I couldn't please my husband . . ." I shook my head and felt tears squeeze themselves out of the corners of my eyes and roll down my face. I wiped them away but had the feeling that they wouldn't be the last to appear. The gin had quickly opened my emotional valve.

"I know how hate and fear can paralyze you," Miriam said. "They had a hold on me for a long time. I hated my father and mother and Mr. Radu for what they did to my childhood. Then I hated my boyfriend and his cousin for what they made me do. I eventually decided I needed to reshape my life, and I found a new family. You met a lot of them at the baby shower. We celebrate each other when things go right and pick each other up when things go wrong."

"You mean with clients?"

"Sometimes with clients, but life in general can go terribly wrong for everyone. I have developed deep ties with many of the women in our community. Like I said, pain and suffering can end up creating bonds. When one of our own is in pain, we come together. Like with May." She paused then sighed sadly. "One day, May spotted her younger sister, Gaia, in the district with a group of low lives. She had sent money home to Thailand for years and specifically instructed her mother to use that money for Gaia's education. As you know, May's older sister had been brought here before her, and May wanted to break the chain of trafficking in her family. Seeing her younger sister was shocking. She chased her down and when she got closer, she could see that Gaia's arms were full of track marks. Heroin. Gaia didn't even recognize her, and when May tried to remove her from the group, one pulled a knife on her. She followed them for a while but lost them in the throng of people and never saw Gaia again. It upset May so much that for a while, we were worried that she would take her own life, so we spent a lot of time with her, supporting her and helping her regain hope. She has experienced a lot of sadness."

I blinked. "Wow, that's quite a story. I never would have guessed. She has such a calm and peaceful way about her."

"Yes, we all have our stories, and they are ours to write. We can fill them with love or hate." Miriam paused to sip her gin, and I watched her hold the alcohol in her mouth before she swallowed slowly, head back and eyes closed.

"So, what will you write for yourself, Beth? Tomorrow is Christmas. A perfect day to begin your new story."

Miriam was right. It was time for me to make some decisions. I hadn't been idle about exploring ideas over the last few days. Using Miriam's computer, I'd done some research and found that I could apply for a work visa and get a job in a café or a store. Maybe the owner of Les Petites Chattes could use a helper? Miriam had told me that a work visa could take up to ninety days to arrive, but I hoped that she'd allow me to pay her back if my money ran out—and if she'd have me for that long. I could also do some online sales work that wouldn't require a work visa. I'd save money and keep considering my options. Miriam kept telling me to focus only on tomorrow, though. "Getting too far ahead of yourself could cloud your vision," she'd said. "One day at a time."

It was good advice.

Still, the options kept appearing in my mind. I could look into childcare—there were lots of little ones in this city. Hell, I could even choose to rent a window if I decided to stay indefinitely! The thought made me chuckle. I certainly had a lot of lost time to make up for in that area.

While Dennis wasn't in my plans for the future, Troy certainly was. I had to figure out my next steps with him, but time was on my side in this regard—he'd be at Sunrise for another five months. In my present state, five months was a lifetime.

Tomorrow would be the beginning of my new story. I just knew it.

Miriam and I finished our drinks, exchanged hugs and well-wishes, and headed to our rooms. Not yet tired, I pulled out some paper from the drawer of the small desk and wrote a letter to Troy. I had the address of Sunrise Ranch, and if Dennis tried to keep him from me by moving him, there would be a paper trail to follow. Miriam had reminded me of this.

In the letter, I told Troy my truth and that I'd be in contact with him soon. I knew he wouldn't want to see me right now, maybe not for a long time, but I had to have faith that he'd allow my love for him to surface in his life once again. And when that happened, I'd be there.

As I drifted off to sleep, I thought about the letter I'd left for Dennis on his suitcase. A marker of the end of my old life. It had been all I could muster without conveying anger and loathing:

Dennis,

I have arranged for you to be contacted if something happens to me. If you don't hear anything, I'm fine. Maybe we'll find each other again. I'm closer than you think.

Beth

21

Christmas Day—Again

I woke to a soft knock on my door. "It is Christmas!" Miriam said with a grin as she peeked in. A heavenly mixture of aromas—cinnamon rolls, bacon and eggs, and coffee— wafted in, and I grinned back.

I hopped out of bed with the excitement of a child, feeling joy permeating the flat. We had agreed not to exchange gifts, but I'd wrapped up the porcelain replica of the Oude Kerk I'd bought during my initial three days in Amsterdam and set it under the tree. It seemed appropriate. After all, it was outside this church that I'd first met Miriam, by the bronze statue of the breast in the cobblestones. Had it not been for that moment, I would probably be miserable, at home alone, without hope or dreams.

I was also planning to finish my tulip painting today, and if it turned out nicely, I'd frame it for Miriam so she could hang it in her hallway. There was a perfect spot for it.

"OK, I have a Christmas present for you," she announced, as we finished doing the breakfast dishes. "You need to go shower and get dressed. Wear something pretty. We are going out."

I turned to her with my hands on my hips. "But we agreed no presents," I said, with mock anger.

"I noticed you did not honor the agreement either." She nodded toward the tree with a smirk. "You have thirty minutes. Get a move on."

I showered and then put on my white angora sweater and my black velvet skirt because they were festive. Since it was Christmas Day, I also put on some heels, curled my hair, and added a splash of makeup. I was pleased with my reflection. Somehow, I looked better than I had in years. Or was it simply my new perspective allowing me to see a different image of myself? I glanced at the calendar on the desk. My journey had started with three days in Amsterdam. Those days kick started the beginning of me finding myself. As I looked at the month of December, I counted beyond the three days in Amsterdam, and to my surprise, if you counted today, I realized that I had been here for a total of seventeen days! The irony of that number was uncanny. It took me seventeen years to lose myself and a mere seventeen days to find myself. The thought made me shake my head in disbelief and sparked a sense of hope.

The streets were quiet as we headed out, our arms linked. Miriam explained that most religious families in the city attended church, both on Christmas Eve and Christmas morning. The bells rang in the distance.

"Where are we going?"

"Be patient and trust me. You trust me, yes?" She looked at me and cocked her head.

I laughed. "Yes, of course, but what's with all this mystery? I'm not good at surprises."

"Well, the new Beth will have to be better at surprises. OK?"

I nodded. I could get on board with that. As the Oude Kerk's dome came into sight, I asked, "Are you taking me to church?" I didn't feel prepared for that.

"No, no church. Unless you would like to go? There are probably no seats left and the service is in Dutch. Maybe next year when your Dutch is better?" She squeezed my arm and we continued.

"So was it hard to learn Dutch? It sounds like a difficult language to learn."

"You would be surprised how fast you can learn a language when your back is up against the wall. English is just as difficult." She winked at me.

"That makes you trilingual: Romanian, Dutch, and English. Any other languages you know that I haven't discovered?" I asked, marveling that she spoke three languages like it was second nature to her.

"Not unless you count the language of love… that is my most fluent language." She smiled at me as we pressed on, "But we will have you speaking Dutch in no time! You will see!"

We passed the ground sculpture of the breast and then *Belle*, near the church entrance. Now that I understood their purpose, they felt so much more important. I wanted to understand my purpose as well.

When we turned left by the church, I could see bodies pressed up against the doorway, hoping for a glimpse of the service in session. Organ music permeated the air.

"Are we going to the Red Light District?" I was seriously confused now, but Miriam nudged me on. This was the last place I'd thought I'd find myself today. There was a sense of calm on the street, as if it were honoring the day as well.

"See that man over there?" She nodded in the direction of Tom's cheese shop, on the other side of the canal.

Standing near the cheese shop, on the almost-empty street, was a striking man. He was tall, well-built and had salt-and-pepper hair and tan skin.

"He's gorgeous," I said quietly. "Do you know him?"

"OK, keep walking and listen to me."

We passed her window, and he watched us as if he knew exactly where we were going. I kept looking at him. His smile was kind.

"Where are we going, Miriam?"

We rounded the corner after passing the whiskey shop and the shop that advertised magic mushrooms in its window, and then she stopped at the crest of the canal bridge that would take us out of the Red Light District, turned to me, and took my hands. A light snow had begun to sprinkle down on us gently, like ash from a fire. It didn't feel cold enough for snow, but this morning didn't seem to be an ordinary morning.

"For Christmas, I am giving you the gift of choice," Miriam said, as she looked deep into my eyes.

I frowned a little "What do you mean? Do you want me to jump off this bridge? That isn't exactly my idea of starting fresh—"

"That man you saw is Robert."

My eyebrows rose. "Robert? Your Robert? Why didn't we stop to say hi? I'd love to meet him." I pulled on her arm, but she pulled me back.

"No, he is not here to see me."

I frowned. "Really? You didn't say he visited other women."

"Listen to me." She took my face in her hands to demand my focus. "I know you are struggling to find your way and I know you are hurting. I know you question your womanhood and your worthiness. I know you are angry. All of that takes time to heal. But today, I am giving you the gift of choice," she repeated. "You may choose what you want to do and why you want to do it or not do it and what you want to do once it is done."

"You've lost me completely, Miriam. What's going on?"

Miriam dropped her hands from my face, took my right hand, and pressed a key in my palm, closing my fingers around it.

"I am giving you time with Robert for Christmas." She shook her head and smiled, seeing the expression of utter shock and horror on my face. "Before you say anything, hear me out. You have choices. We always have choices. You can go into my window and talk to Robert about Dennis. You can go into my window and talk to Robert about moving forward in life. You can go into my window and talk to him about Troy. You can go into my window and let Robert pleasure you. He is giving you this choice as well. He knows your story. The point is that you have the choice. You are in control. It cannot get any simpler. Today, you have the power to choose what you want or need. It took me a long time to gain this power. This is the greatest gift I can offer you.

"Now," she continued, "you are going to walk around the corner and unlock my door. He will follow you in. Whatever you choose will be the right thing for you. Do you understand me?" She squeezed my hand more tightly around the key. "I want you to have what you need, Beth. I want you to be able to release yourself from the lies and the anger of your past, so you can move forward. We will never speak of your choice. It is just for you to know. Trust yourself. I believe this will be the first step in the right direction for you. Merry Christmas."

She leaned in and kissed my cheek and, before I could say a word, turned and walked away, calling, "You know the way home." Her hand went up in a wave, but she didn't turn around.

For a moment, I couldn't move. My head was spinning. A dribble of people made their way through the Red Light District. Some curtains had been pulled shut. This place offered sex but also love. It was a community. It was a hustle and a refuge. It was a place of business and opportunity. It was a place of belonging.

I felt oddly free as I finally made my way to Miriam's window.

Robert was still standing on the other side of the bridge. He tipped his felt cap in acknowledgment when I looked his way. His smile suggested he'd seen into my soul and held the key to unlocking my new path. I kept Miriam's words in mind. I had no idea what was about to transpire as I approached the glass door, but whatever happened would be my choice. That was what I needed to focus on.

I felt as if I were a dandelion head hosting hundreds of barely connected seeds ready to take flight and disappear as soon as the wind picked up. The seeds were my past: the father who'd abandoned me, the mother who'd underestimated me, the higher education that had eluded me, the husband who'd betrayed me, the son who'd lost faith in me, the acquaintances who'd never taken an interest in me, the house that had taken hostage of me, the choices that had served to hide me from myself. All these seeds were losing their grip on me.

As if on command, a breeze blew down the street, whipping up tiny, delicate snowflakes. I caught sight of them in the glass of Miriam's window, rising and dancing away in the wind, taking with them the weight of the past and making way for the future.

It was a mere change in perspective.

I smiled, trusting that the Christmas gift that awaited

me on the other side of the glass door would possibly be the best I'd ever received.

The first time I'd looked in the glass door, I'd seen what was on the other side and been appalled. Now, as I stood firmly planted, I saw everything around me, swirling in currents, a petri dish of life waiting to be examined. The image was fluid and ever-changing. It couldn't be held, only observed and appreciated or reviled. I decided to appreciate it.

And then, reflected in the glass—a pair of eyes not my own. They were blue, the color of a calm sea, and they latched on to my gaze, warming the very space where I stood. The power of the connection stunned me, yet I didn't turn around. Instead, I relied on my senses to carry me along. I closed my eyes like an old cat and inhaled deeply. Then I opened them slowly as I exhaled. The other set of eyes hadn't disappeared. They were still there, patiently waiting. True to my new, reflective self, I paused to consider the possible effects of my choice. My next move held the promise that my life would never be the same. How could I go wrong?

I reached for the knob and, with no further thoughts, stepped through the door.

Three Days in Amsterdam
Book Club Questions for Discussion

1. Before reading this story, did you have any preconceived notions about the Red Light District in Amsterdam? What were they? Have your beliefs about the district changed or stayed the same?

2. Prostitution exists all over the world. What makes the Red Light District so unique?

3. Why do you think Beth and Miriam were able to develop a deep friendship in such a short period?

4. Given the type of person Dennis is, do you believe that Beth could have done anything differently in her marriage to avoid losing herself in it?

5. What do you think Beth does after she steps into Miriam's window at the end of the story?

6. Do you think that Beth and Troy will be able to repair their relationship in the future? What steps might need to be taken?

7. What do you think Beth will do next with her life?

Acknowledgements

It is safe to say that many hands helped shape this novel. With the hard work of my editor, Rachel Small, we were able to bring this story to life. Her attention to detail and story momentum helped streamline my original manuscript. She helped me develop the best version of my writing and I feel honored to have worked with her on both of my novels.

Another big thanks goes to David Provolo, the cover designer and formatter of both of my books. His gift to create a visual that captures the essence of my writing is second to none. I am humbled to be working with him.

Without the encouragement to write, which came from my mother and teachers throughout my early years, I may not have found this medium of expression that has served me well. Writing is definitely a form of therapy for me and will always be my way of processing life, factual as well as fictional.

Finally, I thank my family. My children have offered me a wealth of subject matter to write about and I many times tap into those in order to convey certain scenes in my book. My husband, Jim, has been by my side encouraging me for decades to chase my dream of publishing books. For forty years, he has been my tech guy, my beta reader, my cheerleader, and my relentless supporter. Without him, I may not have been able to pull this off. I am forever indebted to him. And last, to my readers, thank you for being willing to take a chance on my novels. I hope they offer you what you are looking for. Read on!!!

About the Author

Three Days in Amsterdam is Tanja Tucker's second novel, published in 2023. Her first novel, *The Garnet Earrings* was published in August 2022. Seeing her novel on the shelves of bookstores, available on line, and in the hands of readers was always a dream of hers. Tanja has two adult children, resides in California with her husband, where she continues to explore life through travel and the written word, seeking inspiration for unique storylines.

Made in the USA
Monee, IL
27 March 2025

14751923R00154